The Boiling Sea

Brass and Glass, Book 3

Dawn Vogel

Cover Art by J. Kathleen Cheney

DEDICATION

To everyone who has been waiting for this book. Here it is!

Books in the Brass & Glass Series

The Cask of Cranglimmering
The Long-Cursed Map
The Boiling Sea

CONTENTS

CHAPTER ONE

Captain Svetlana Tereshchenko of *The Silent Monsoon* paused on the trail, glancing ahead toward the prison fortress of Aldfort, and then looking back to the spot where her airship had dropped off her and the ship's doctor, Annette Campbell. "Couldn't they have gotten us any closer?" she grumbled.

Ahead of Svetlana, Annette chuckled, turning her head so Svetlana could hear her voice clearly, as the winds sweeping across the broad plain whipped tendrils of her dark curly hair across her flushed brown face. "Could have, yes, if you didn't mind your ship getting a warning shot or three. Some of which might have been less 'warning shot' and more 'shot.'"

"Then at least the prison could've sent a carriage for us."

"I have to assume my letter offering my services didn't arrive ahead of us," Annette said. "Either that, or they're certain Doctor Jacquelina Morton is not a real person." Annette sighed. "Did we have to go with Jacquelina?"

"It'll have to do. Doctor Morton," Svetlana said, trying out the name to remind herself of Annette's alias. It felt strange in her mouth. Though Svetlana had not known Annette when she wasn't a doctor, Annette had never stood on ceremony. The doctor asked Svetlana to call her Annette, rather than Doctor Campbell, from the first time her late husband, Jack, had introduced the two of them.

"Let's just hope the staff brings us Jo quickly, and the gents can get here as fast as Athos says they can," Annette said.

Athos, Svetlana's first mate, and Indigo, the ship's mechanic, had remained onboard *The Silent Monsoon* to await a signal from Svetlana and Annette. Svetlana jostled the small cage hidden under her cloak and received an annoyed squawk from the crow inside.

While she thought a pigeon was the appropriate bird for taking a message back to the *Monsoon*, when the Crow Man, a noble in Heliopolis who had connections to Indigo's friend Deliah, had presented her with the gift of a homing crow, she had accepted.

As Svetlana and Annette reached the prison gates, the guard there, a pale woman with loose skin sagging from her skull much as her ill-fitting clothing sagged around her rail-thin body, squinted at the two women. "You the doc?" she asked, her voice gravelly.

"I am," Annette said. "Doctor Jacquelina Morton. My assistant, Maud."

Svetlana nodded in turn when her alias was mentioned, careful to keep her hood pulled down low enough to cover her eyes. Though a simple eyepatch covered her blind eye, there was little she could do to cover the amber-gold of her good eye, a feature that had been publicized during the Air Fleet's campaign to locate her and her crew.

The guard hesitated just long enough to make Svetlana start to worry that their cover story would not get them into the prison. Svetlana began considering alternatives to getting through impenetrable walls from the ground, though she knew such an approach was impossible. Aldfort was perched atop a high outcropping of rock without even space for a footpath around the exterior walls. The crew had dismissed any ideas of an aerial assault before they began planning for this endeavor, as guard towers ensured the prison's early notification of any such approach. Through the front door with a cover story was the best way in.

Finally, the guard said, "Very good, we'll take you to the infirmary, and then we'll bring you the ill and injured prisoners."

"How many are we expected to see today?" Annette asked. "The information I received was incomplete."

"Dozen or so," the guard replied listlessly. "Never know how many sick and broken sods we'll have any given day."

Svetlana and Annette were counting on Jo to be among the injured. The *Monsoon*'s pilot had been captured sneaking into the chambers of the High Council, where she'd hoped to get information from the three Cranglimmering whiskey casks the Republic had collected over the years.

A reproduction of the cask staves had been in the possession of Lady Elinor de Whittvy, now deceased, who had seen the originals in the High Council's chambers some time ago. But in the course of collecting additional staves, and the pieces of the map inscribed upon them, Svetlana and her crew had discovered that Lady de Whittvy might have missed some key elements. The crew of *The Silent Monsoon* had recently learned the map hidden in the seven whiskey casks was referred to as the "Long-Cursed" map, and it was said to point to the location of the Last Emperor's Hoard, a treasure beyond measure, which included, among other valuable pieces, the Gem of the Seas. And the Gem of the Seas was said to allow its bearer to control the oceans.

Since the oceans had been boiling for more than five centuries, several organizations or entities now sought the treasure and, consequently, the map that would lead to it. The Air Fleet, the military arm of the Republic, was among that number. More surprising was the interest of a coalition of ghosts who flew their ghostly ships in and out of Aetherwhere, a place long believed to be the home of the Faerie Queen, whom no one had met.

The guard led Svetlana and Annette into the prison, taking them to a small room with a low cot and stool on one side of the room, and a small table on the other side. It smelled clean and antiseptic here, much like the infirmary on *The Silent Monsoon*, though there was a faint underlying odor of the sulfurous ocean air.

After both Svetlana and Annette were in the room, the guard spoke again, gesturing to a second door in the room. "Your prisoners will come in through there with a guard or two apiece. If you anticipate you'll be staying overnight, we'll take you to a place where you can sleep."

"Oh, we do hope not," Annette said, barely hiding her distaste at the thought of spending a night behind bars, even in a portion of the prison reserved for a doctor and her assistant.

The guard nodded. "Then I'll see you when you're through." She pulled the door shut with a clang, then slid what sounded like a bar into place.

A cold sweat broke out on the back of Svetlana's neck. Annette had spent a night in jail not too many months back. Svetlana, despite the odds, never had, her loyalty to the Air Fleet in her younger years keeping her out of the sort of trouble she might have found otherwise. Already, she felt penned in by this small treatment room.

The second door opened, and Svetlana had to disguise her disappointment that the prisoner was a manacled elderly man, bloodshot green eyes darting around, with a mane of wiry black and gray hair and beard, as a pair of burly male guards, both possessed of the sort of sun-and-wind-tanned skin that was common among people who spent significant time outdoors, escorted him in.

"This is Alfred," one of the guards said. "He bites. So if you've got a head restraint in that bag of yours, I'd use it."

Annette nodded, her eyes wide, and rummaged in her bag without a word.

~

Over a dozen patients and their assorted guards came through Annette's makeshift infirmary before the guards brought Jo in. Her normally shining long auburn hair was plaited into a thick, matted braid. Her gaze was downcast, her pale skin sallow, and she looked as though she'd lost far more weight than Svetlana would have thought a person could lose in just a couple of weeks.

"Name?" Annette asked before either guard could speak.

Jo looked up, recognition crossing her features, then tucked her chin low again.

One of the guards, distinguishable from the other only by his lighter colored hair, said, "She's the notorious pirate, Josephine Dean."

"Pirate?" Svetlana asked, pitching her voice softer than normal.

"Oh, aye," the guard said. "Charged with grand high treason, on account of breaking and entering at the High Council's chambers."

"I don't care about what she's done," Annette said, the faintest tremble in her words. "What's wrong with her?"

"Broken jaw," the guard replied. "Doesn't know how to hold her tongue."

Svetlana forced herself to bite back her temper, grinding her molars together. The faint yellowing around Jo's jawline suggested the injury was older, possibly sustained prior to arriving at the prison, but it could have been a beating at the hands of these very guards, or others like them. She flicked a glance in Annette's direction and noticed the doctor, too, was breathing slowly and evenly through her flared nostrils.

"Let's see what we can do, then," Annette said, taking Jo's hand and leading her to the low cot. "Has she been eating?"

"Broth, mostly," the darker-haired guard spoke up. "On account of the jaw."

"How long has she had this injury?" Annette asked, gently holding up Jo's chin so she could look into her eyes.

"Came here with it," the first guard replied.

Annette spun to glare at him. "And she hasn't been seen prior to today?"

The lighter-haired guard shrugged. "Our old doc's been gone the whole time. Good thing you came by here."

Annette turned back to Jo and ran her hands gingerly along either side of Jo's jawline. For her part, Jo managed to remain still, though she winced a bit, and a tear slid from the corner of one eye. "She's got an infection, on account of the bone not setting properly. I'm going to need to sedate her and see if I can reset the bone."

"Who cares if her bone's not set right?" the same guard asked.

"She expected to go to trial?" Annette asked.

He shrugged again. "Her hands aren't broken."

Svetlana stepped between the lighter-haired guard and Annette, her expression as neutral as she could make it. She kept the softer tone in her voice but spoke forcefully. "Sir, I respectfully suggest you let Doctor Morton do her job."

The guards looked at each other. The lighter-haired one who had been arguing against fixing Jo's jaw shook his head, but the darker-haired one spoke up. "She's the last patient today, so you've got about an hour. Do what you can."

Annette looked up, a smile crossing her face. "An hour should be sufficient."

The lighter-haired guard left the room, but the other lingered behind.

Svetlana glanced back at Annette, then to the guard. "Sir, if you need to attend to other prisoners, we'll be fine here. She'll be sedated shortly."

The guard shook his head. "No guards in the room is against policy."

"What are your feelings on blood and pus?" Annette asked, pinning him with her gaze.

The guard blanched. "Point taken. If you need assistance, bang on this door."

Svetlana nodded curtly, and the guard slipped out of the room.

"Thank the Skyfather," Annette muttered under her breath.

"Indeed," Svetlana said. She placed her hand on Jo's shoulder. "We found you."

Jo gave a small nod, tears now streaming from her eyes.

"Give her the good stuff, Doc," Svetlana said, fumbling under her cloak for the crow's cage. She pulled it out and set the cage on the high windowsill, then unlatched the door.

The crow hesitated a moment, as though taking stock of its surroundings and getting its bearings, before it launched itself into the sky beyond.

~

When the darker-haired guard came back into the infirmary, he didn't look closely at Jo, who was covered head to toe with a white sheet. "Doc?"

Annette looked up, her dark eyes solemn. "My apologies, sir. The patient's injuries were more substantial than were apparent on my initial examination. It's proven to be too much for her body to handle."

The guard nodded. "I see. I'll—I'll make the necessary arrangements, then."

Annette gave a quick nod, and the guard withdrew. As soon as he was out of sight, she pulled the sheet off Jo's sleeping face and looked at Svetlana. "How much longer until Athos gets here? If anyone with half a lick of sense looks at Jo, they'll see she's still breathing."

Svetlana peered out the window. "Soon, I hope. How fast do crows fly?"

"Not fast enough," Annette murmured.

Metal scraped on metal on the other side of the door Svetlana and Annette had come through, as though the bar was being lifted from the door.

"Cover her back up," Svetlana whispered, moving to interpose herself between Jo and whoever came through the door.

A heavyset woman with a narrow, aquiline nose peered at Svetlana and Annette through a dainty pair of glasses. "The guards inform me the prisoner is dead?"

Svetlana took in a deep breath, ready to defend Annette, but before she could speak, a klaxon sounded.

6

"Warning! Turn back your ship!" The announcement was loud enough to vibrate Svetlana's bones as she stumbled to maintain her balance.

The woman in the doorway braced herself against the doorframe, then exhaled audibly. "I'll return shortly," she said, turning and stomping away.

Svetlana hazarded a glance out the infirmary window. It took her a moment to make sense of what she saw. It wasn't *The Silent Monsoon* that approached, but a newer, sleeker ship, one with silvery gray balloons and flying a flag she didn't recognize. The ship looked like a Kavisoli ship, belonging to the former crime family turned governors of the city-state of Rrusadon, and led by Svetlana's paramour, Mayor Larson Kavisoli. But the flag was not that of Rrusadon.

A voice boomed out, not half as loud as the warning announcement from Aldfort. "We come on behalf of the Taedmorden family, and demand audience with your administrator at his or her earliest convenience, which we hope will also coincide with *our* earliest convenience."

The distortion from the amplification disguised Athos's voice at first, but Svetlana grinned when she recognized it. "Get her ready to travel, Doc. Ship's here."

"That's not our ship," Annette said, peering out the window.

"Nope, it's one of Lar's. Skyfather knows why he decided to get tangled up in this after I asked him nicely to let us handle it. Also why Athos agreed to a change in plans."

"Well, anyone within earshot is going to have an aneurism trying to figure out how the Taedmordens and the Kavisolis are connected, if they put the ship and the flag together," Annette said as she tucked the edges of the sheet under the mattress upon which Jo lay.

"Oh, is that the Taedmorden crest?" Svetlana asked. "I'm a little surprised Athos agreed to fly under it."

"Needs must," Annette replied. "You got a plan for getting us out of here?"

Svetlana nodded. "Same plan we came in with. We've gotta go up."

"Up?" Annette cocked her head to the side and stared at Svetlana. "How do you plan to get an unconscious Jo anywhere that involves up?"

"To be fair, I didn't realize we'd need to knock her out when we made this plan." Looking around the room, Svetlana seized upon two brooms, both of which had seen better days. "Stretcher. Stick these under the mattress and lash the whole thing together."

"That'll work fine, Captain, at least until we run into the spiral staircase that takes us up into the tower," Annette said, accepting one of the brooms and beginning to prepare the makeshift stretcher.

"We'll deal with it when we get there," Svetlana said.

As soon as she and Annette had the poles in place, they each took one end of the stretcher and headed out into the prison hallways. Most of the prison staff had moved to locations where they could see the incoming airship, which seemed likely to be pelted with cannon balls at any moment. That Aldfort had not yet opened fire on the Kavisoli ship was a bit of a surprise, but Svetlana didn't have time to consider the implications.

She and Annette moved through the hallways swiftly but didn't run, lest they draw too much attention to themselves. They kept Jo's face covered, so it looked to the casual observer as though they were carrying a corpse to whatever passed for a morgue in this prison.

The problem was that most morgues were kept below ground, not above.

"Where are you going?" a dark brown skinned guard asked as they headed toward the tower at the northeast corner of the prison. This guard was surprisingly small and lithe compared to the others they'd seen.

Svetlana scrambled for an answer, stammering through the beginning of a few sentences. "She's, uhhh, I mean to say, we're going to—"

"We need to take her into a better lit portion of the prison so I can do a post-mortem examination," Annette said, her voice smooth and even where Svetlana's had been panicky and high-pitched.

The guard narrowed his gaze for a moment before nodding and letting the women pass.

"Good thinking, Doc," Svetlana murmured as they continued toward the tower.

"Your turn next, then," Annette replied as they reached the anticipated spiral staircase that led into the tower where Athos was supposed to be picking them up in *The Silent Monsoon*. "How do we get Jo up those stairs?"

Svetlana checked the hallway behind them. None of the guards were looking in their direction, as most were gawking out the windows at the inbound ship. Pulling a well-concealed knife from her boot, Svetlana slit the bindings they had used to keep the stretcher poles in place and slipped her arms under Jo's still body. The pilot, despite her slender build, was heavier than Svetlana was prepared to carry on her own, but she cradled Jo in her arms and gestured at the staircase with her chin. "Go."

~

From the top of the watchtower, Svetlana could see for miles. Below, the Kavisoli ship hovered just inside the range of the cannon at Aldfort, but so far, no shots had been fired. The skies around the tower, however, were dishearteningly empty, aside from a few puffy white clouds.

"Where's our pickup?" Svetlana muttered.

Annette reached where Svetlana was standing and scanned the skies. "Not here," she said, reaching out to take Jo from Svetlana's aching arms.

"Sure, now you'll carry her, after five flights of stairs."

"You seemed like you had it under control, Captain, and far be it from me to doubt your strength." Annette smiled at Svetlana in a way that might seem patronizing coming from anyone else. Svetlana knew the doctor was being genuine.

"Well, I guess we wait, then." Svetlana looked around the tower. "Maybe lean Jo over there, against the wall?"

A clattering from below covered any response Annette might have made. Svetlana ran to the top of the stairs that led to this watchtower. Pounding footsteps followed from somewhere down the stairs.

"We've got incoming," Svetlana said, pulling her guns out from beneath her loose-fitting shirt. "I'm going to need help."

"You want me to fight?" Annette asked, her eyebrows knitting together.

"No, but I might need your weapons."

"I didn't bring any," Annette said.

"Really?" Svetlana asked, blinking at Annette. "Then check for Jo's."

Annette returned Svetlana's dumbfounded look. "She's been in prison."

"If you search her body and don't come up with a single weapon, I might die of shock, Doctor Campbell."

"Point taken," Annette said, turning back to where she had propped Jo into a corner.

Svetlana turned back to the stairs in time to spot the first of their pursuers coming around the last curve in the staircase. She aimed both her pistols toward the woman in the lead. "Hi there," she said with a grin, fingers on the triggers.

"Halt!" the guard said, holding up her left hand, fist clenched, as a signal to her troops.

"How about you halt on back down those stairs?" Svetlana suggested.

The guard steeled herself, her gaze boring straight into Svetlana. "You are charged with aiding and abetting the escape of a prisoner of the High Council—"

Svetlana lowered one of her guns and fired at the guard's leg.

The shot hit the guard's thigh solidly, and she screamed, clutching at the wound.

"Captain, is there any possibility we know anyone who can fly a cloud?" Annette asked.

It took a moment for Svetlana to parse what Annette had asked, and even then, she wasn't sure what the doctor meant. "Fly a cloud?"

"There's a rather substantial cloud making its way toward us at a faster than your average cloud pace."

Svetlana arched an eyebrow but kept her pistols trained on the lead guard. "Still want to arrest me?" she asked.

The guard whimpered in response. A pair of her compatriots seemed to be attempting to pass the wounded guard down the stairs.

Svetlana shifted her aim to the legs of each of those guards and fired.

Again, her shots were met with screams, and the lead guard tumbled out of her troops' grasp.

"Why don't you people put doors on your towers?" she grumbled. With the situation on the stairs temporarily contained,

Svetlana hazarded a glance at the sky. She, too, saw a massive cloud moving toward the tower at a quick clip. The water vapor swirled in a hypnotic, unnatural pattern, and Svetlana cocked her head to the side. Then, for the briefest of moments, there was a glimmer of red at the top of the cloud, and she grinned. She'd recognize the bright red "rose" balloon on her ship anywhere.

"It's the *Monsoon*," she told Annette.

A rope ladder fell from the cloud as it came to rest above the tower, obscuring the view from the staircase with billowing warm mist.

"Indy?" Svetlana called up into the cloud.

A bright blue mop of hair appeared in the mist, framing a face nearly as white as the cloud itself. "Hi, Captain!"

"Jo's sick. We're going to need to haul her up. Go grab the winch."

Indigo nodded, his hair bobbing around his face like its own little cloud before he vanished again.

"Up you go, Doc," Svetlana said. "Help Indy rig up something to get Jo onboard." She took a step backward, the cloud now blocking her view of the doorway at the top of the stairs. Muffled voices came from beyond the doorway, indistinct enough that she couldn't tell if they were approaching or leaving.

Annette scaled the ladder, her doctor's bag slung over her shoulder to give her full use of her limbs for climbing. Muffled voices came from above, now, and the ladder jerked as two figures made their way down.

Svetlana recognized the new arrivals as Kavisolis, based on their superficial family resemblance to Lar—dark hair, olive skin, and physically fit—but she wasn't sure of their names.

"Doc says you've got an injured pilot down here?" the taller of the two asked.

Svetlana nodded and pointed at Jo's prone body.

The Kavisoli scoffed. "Why'd she send two of us for that little thing?"

"That little thing is the best damn pilot I've ever met," Svetlana said. "Handle with care."

The young man nodded sheepishly and picked up Jo, cradling her against his body as though she were an infant. The other man held on to the bottom of the ladder and kept it steady as the man carrying Jo went up.

"After you, Captain," he said, still maintaining his grip on the bottom of the ladder.

Svetlana hazarded one more glance back at the doorway into Aldfort Prison and then climbed the ladder onto her ship.

~

Svetlana made her way directly to the bridge as the cloud-shrouded airship flew away from the tower top. On reaching it, she found several Kavisolis at the helm of her ship.

One of them was Martin, one of Lar's younger cousins who had helped her and her crew with previous endeavors. Though smaller in stature than many of the other Kavisoli cousins, most of whom towered over Svetlana, Martin had proven himself to be a competent fighter and pilot, invaluable to Svetlana when she was in a pinch. He stood in front of a device Svetlana didn't recognize, twisting knobs and toggling a large switch. The device was a good-sized box, still smaller than most of the crates *The Silent Monsoon* normally shipped, set on a spindly-legged table near the back of the bridge, not too far from the speaking tube that allowed those on the bridge to communicate with those below. It was covered with knobs, gauges, buttons, and the single switch, with several lights flashing on its surface.

"What's this, then?" Svetlana asked, puzzling over the new equipment on the bridge.

"Bride gift," Martin replied with a wide grin.

Svetlana was certain she'd misheard him. "Wha—What?"

Martin paled immediately. "Uhhhh, for ... uhhh. You know what? Pretend I said nothing."

Svetlana shook her head. "There's no bride-ing going on, Martin."

"No, of course not." He forced a laugh. "Who would have said such a ridiculous thing? I mean clearly, no one of the marrying sort around here."

"Clearly," Svetlana said. But the implications were unmistakable. Martin was under the impression that his cousin had asked Svetlana to marry him. Lar had done no such thing. If he had, Svetlana would have turned him down. She'd spent thirty-seven years without ever becoming irrevocably attached to another person, and she wasn't about to change that now. Lar had to know as much, based on the conversations they had had, but if he was sending strange devices to her ship, along with his family members as supplementary crew, she could only suspect that perhaps he thought he'd try to win her over to making such a commitment with him.

"How about I tell you what it does?" Martin asked.

"Generates the cloud, I'd daresay?"

Martin nodded. "Or you can just guess correctly, and I'll go back to getting us out of here."

"Sounds like a plan," Svetlana replied.

CHAPTER TWO

Svetlana stood beside Martin on the horizontal controls as they guided *The Silent Monsoon* into dock at the floating platform city of Rrusadon. They'd spoken little after Martin's gaffe regarding his cousin's intentions.

As the ship settled on its docking struts, Svetlana locked the horizontal controls and moved to leave the bridge.

"Captain," Martin said.

She turned back to look at him, arching one eyebrow.

"Go easy on Lar."

"Tell me one thing," she said, her voice quiet. "Did he call it a bride gift or did you?"

"Oh, I did," Martin said, but the skin twitching between his eyebrows told Svetlana he was likely lying.

She forced a smile. "Then I'll be nice." It was only fair to repay his lie with one of her own. She left the bridge and started the small motor they used to lower the gangplank.

The Kavisoli ship that had been outside Aldfort Prison pulled into a docking slip next to *The Silent Monsoon*. Athos stood at the front of the ship and was waving his arms wildly to get Svetlana's attention.

Checking that the gangplank was aligned correctly to allow her to depart the ship when fully lowered, Svetlana moved toward the stern of *The Silent Monsoon* to get nearer to the other ship.

"We may have been followed," Athos shouted.

Svetlana's good eye widened, and she ran back to the bridge. "Spyglass!" she shouted as soon as she opened the door.

Martin grabbed the requested item and hurried over to her, carrying it as carefully as he could.

"It's a hearty one," Svetlana said as she accepted the device from him. "Toss it next time."

"Next time?" Martin forced a stiff smile.

"We'll see," Svetlana replied. She hurried back out onto the deck and scanned the skies to the north, the direction they'd just come from. She called out to Athos, "What am I looking for?"

"Fast moving cloud," he shouted.

Svetlana shook her head. "That was the *Monsoon*."

"No, there was another one, I think. Or maybe I'm just being paranoid."

Svetlana moved the spyglass across the broad expanse of blue sky more slowly, pausing as she came across any clouds. Though plenty of small white spots peppered the sky, none of them appeared to be moving any differently than she might have expected. "I don't see anything."

"Then maybe I was wrong," Athos said. "How's Jo?"

"No word from the Doc yet, and I'm taking that to mean 'still sleeping,'" Svetlana said, lowering the spyglass and looking across the space between the two ships. "You coming over here, or are we just going to shout back and forth all day?"

Athos nodded, running his hands through his short sandy brown hair, just now reaching the length where some of his curls were coming back. He'd cut it previously when they'd been attempting to keep a low profile in Heliopolis a couple of months previous.

Svetlana was a little surprised Athos hadn't torn most of his remaining hair out at this point; he'd spent many long nights with his hands in his hair fretting over Jo's whereabouts. Now that his sometimes lover was back onboard *The Silent Monsoon*, Svetlana hoped Athos would be able to relax and perhaps get a bit more sleep.

"Do you think Doc will mind if I poke my head in?" Athos asked.

Before Svetlana could answer, Martin's voice came through the speaking tube from the bridge of *The Silent Monsoon*. "Captain, Doctor Campbell just called up from below."

Athos broke into a run for the Kavisoli ship's gangplank.

Svetlana began to run toward the stairs but stopped and waited for Athos to join her. They both had plenty of questions for Jo, but this time, Svetlana was willing to let Athos get his questions asked first. As he came onboard, she tilted her head toward the stairs. "Do you want me to give the two of you a moment?"

"Doc's still there," he said, his voice strained. "We'll get our moment later. I want to know what she found out too."

Svetlana squeezed her first mate's shoulders, then pulled him into an awkward hug. Neither of them was really the hugging type, at least not with each other, and it felt like trying to comfort a sibling who really didn't want the gesture.

Athos' muscles were rigid beneath Svetlana's grasp, but he patted her lightly on the back. "Yeah, okay. Let's go, Cap."

Svetlana nodded and led the way down the stairs to the small infirmary they maintained on *The Silent Monsoon*.

Inside, Jo was finally sitting upright, her long auburn hair fanned out to one side, where Annette was gently working out some of the knotted portions of her braid. A wide strip of gauze was tied around her head, holding her jaw up, and a second piece of gauze wrapped from her chin around the back of her head, keeping her jaw from moving forward or backward. Jo's skin was still paler than it normally was, except for some bruising that peeked out from beneath the gauze along her jawline.

As soon as Jo saw Svetlana, she forced a timid smile, which widened when Athos pushed Svetlana forward into the infirmary, rushing over to Jo's side.

Athos's hands fluttered nervously, and he looked at Annette. "Can I hug her, kiss her?"

"Hug, gently," Annette said. "Kiss her forehead, if you like."

Athos gingerly placed his hands on Jo's temples and gave her a delicate kiss on her forehead. "Thank the Skyfather you're back."

Jo made no audible response, but tears flowed down her cheeks.

Svetlana looked between Jo and Annette. "Can she not talk?"

Annette shook her head. "I wasn't lying to those guards when I said her jaw hadn't set right. There's no infection, but I had to reset it on the way back. The gauze should help it heal correctly, since I can't do much more than that without a proper surgery area. It's going to be a while before she's chewing our ears off again."

Jo chuckled, a sound that rumbled in her chest with her mouth still closed, but the sound cut off abruptly with a pained intake of breath through her nostrils. She tapped Athos's chest and pointed toward a notebook on one of Annette's work tables.

"Oh, great, she's going to write us a sonnet," Athos said, rolling his eyes but with a broad grin on his face. He retrieved the notebook for Jo, along with a pencil. "This isn't one of your important notebooks, is it, Doc?"

"No, I brought that one in here for this exact purpose," Annette said.

Jo scribbled in the notebook for a moment, then handed it to Athos.

Reading from the notebook, Athos said, "She says she's seen the map, and there is writing on it, but it's not directions. It's a poem." He looked up and grimaced. "I was kidding about the sonnets, Jo Dean!"

Jo took the notebook back and began writing, more slowly this time, tapping the end of the pencil on the paper occasionally, brow furrowed in thought.

Svetlana took the opportunity to turn her attention to Annette. "I'm guessing she shouldn't be flying the *Monsoon* until she's recovered a bit more?"

"That would be my recommendation, Captain," Annette said. "I'd like to try to keep her pain under control, and you aren't going to want her flying with the kind of drugs I'm going to get for her."

Athos chuckled. "Well, then let's get extras and just hang out here for a while."

Svetlana shook her head. "Let's see this poetry first. You got it all yet, Jo?"

Jo's eyebrows pulled together more, as the sides of her mouth turned down slightly, and she shook her head. She scribbled a few more words, then handed the notebook back to Athos.

"'The Skyfather alone controls the Air, but whosoever controls the Gem controls the Sea. Were the Oceans to cease ... Geysers would turn to ...'" Athos frowned at the page. "That's just awful. It doesn't even rhyme."

Svetlana nodded in agreement. "Are you sure you got this right, Jo?"

Jo nodded once, then shook her head, reaching for the notebook. She scribbled a few more words, then held it up for everyone to see. "'Still missing parts'," it read.

"Alright, if you two want to debate the merits of poetry, take it elsewhere," Annette said. "My patient needs rest." She glanced at

Jo, then back to Svetlana and Athos. "I'll come throw my thoughts in after a bit."

Svetlana nodded and tore the page from the notebook, then handed it back to Jo. "Get better quick, Jo Dean. Else I'm going to wind up yelling at Lar more than is healthy for anyone, and then I'll have to figure out how to hire his cousin to keep this boat in the air till you're better."

Jo rolled her eyes but nodded, giving Svetlana a sloppy salute before the captain left the infirmary.

~

Indigo was on the bridge, tinkering with the device that created clouds, when Svetlana and Athos arrived there with Jo's transcription of the words on the map.

"I find it hard to believe that Lady de Whittvy completely missed the literal writing on the wall." Athos chuckled.

Svetlana smiled in spite of herself, thinking about the charming woman she'd been smitten with. The scientist and noblewoman had been beautiful, intelligent, and possessed of a rebellious spirit, just the sort of person Svetlana was drawn to. However, the timing had not worked out, between Dr. Vertiline Dowhty, Lady Elinor de Whittvy's alter ego, being kidnapped, Svetlana's burgeoning relationship with Lar, and then Vertiline's untimely demise. Svetlana wished she'd had more time to get to know Vertiline.

But that was in the past, and little related to the matter at hand. "The more I think about that, the more I wonder if she saw it, but didn't add it to her version for some reason." Svetlana studied the sheet of paper, then read a bit aloud. "'The Skyfather alone controls the Air.' That's from something, isn't it?"

"The Skyfather alone controls the Air," Indigo piped up. "Any who would usurp his skies are fools."

Athos snapped his fingers. "Yes! Indy, that's it!"

Svetlana looked between the two of them. "Is this some secret code?"

"No, it's a teaching about the Skyfather," Athos said. "I'd be shocked if you never heard it growing up."

With a shrug, Svetlana said, "I didn't really take too well to being taught a lot of things as a kid."

19

Athos's expression bore no evidence of surprise, but he said, "This is my shocked face. Okay, Indy, help me out if I get this wrong." He paused and cleared his throat. "The Skyfather alone controls the Air. Any who would usurp his skies are fools. He lays no claim upon the Sea, for its Mother is fickle and changeable, and the Skyfather blows her waters from his hands."

Indigo chimed in for the second stanza, matching Athos's cadence as though the cadence itself was part of the teaching. "But whosoever controls the Gem controls the Sea, trade and all commerce upon it, the Fleets of the mightiest of warriors, its giving and taking of life, and dominion over the Seamother."

Svetlana clapped when they finished. "Okay, so what does that mean?"

"I don't know that it means anything at all," Athos said. "It's about not claiming dominion over the skies."

"Like one might say the Air Fleet has done?" Svetlana asked, mouth twisting into a wry grin. "Anyway, I suppose I've heard bits of that. My Gran used to say 'Skyfather blow water from my hands' when she didn't want to discuss something further. It was her way of saying she was done with a thing."

Athos chuckled. "I've heard a number of the older crowd say the same thing. I suppose it's an expression that's fallen out of favor."

"It's not complete," Indigo said, peering at the sheet of paper. "See, dots."

Svetlana ruffled Indigo's hair, even though these days, she had to raise her hand almost to her full height to do so. Gone were the days when Indigo only came up to her elbow. Now he threatened to overtop her height on a daily basis, and he wasn't done growing, having celebrated his fourteenth birthday while the crew made plans to rescue Jo from Aldfort. "But it sort of goes together, doesn't it? Were the Oceans to cease, geysers would turn?"

"Turn to what?" Athos asked.

Svetlana shook her head. "I'm not sure. Now that we've got this, we should see if it matches up to any of the bits of writing we've seen. That might answer our questions."

Annette slipped onto the bridge from the back stairway. "Have you got it all figured out already?"

"The first two lines, yes. Athos and Indy knew them," Svetlana said.

Nodding, Annette said, "I recognized them as well. I suspect Jo did too, which is probably why she's got the full lines there, and only part for the other two."

"They read like a warning," Svetlana said. "But without knowing the rest of those lines, we can't be sure what they're warning against."

"Pride?" Indigo asked.

Svetlana cocked her head to the side, and she watched Athos and Annette do the same. "That's quite astute, Indy. Is that what the teaching is about?"

Indigo nodded, his blue hair bouncing up and down with his nods. "Elders said it was a reminder to not become full of pride, or the Skyfather would smite us."

"Your village had an interesting interpretation of the Skyfather," Athos muttered. "But yeah, I suppose that is what it's about."

"Okay, so warn people against pride, and then—" Svetlana trailed off, brow creasing as she looked at the notebook page again. "These are two different things. The first one is something that many people would know and recognize. This second, it's not, right? It's talking about the Gem of the Seas, and what could be done with it, I think."

"That sounds about right," Annette said. "The tone is very different. The first part reads like an old-style teaching, and the second part reads more casually."

"So what do we do with this information?" Athos asked. "I mean, as much as I like the idea of a few weeks of relaxing on Rrusadon while Jo recovers, I imagine that's not the best use of our time."

"Well, we think we know where to look for the Last Emperor's Hoard," Svetlana said. "It means going into the Unfathomed Enclave."

Athos groaned. "Jo's not going to like that."

Svetlana nodded. "I don't either, truth be told, but I don't think it can be avoided. If we're going to have to deal with Dargon, I'd like Jo to be a little more recovered. So maybe our next step is seeing how close we think the Air Fleet or the ghosts might be to having that same information."

"We don't have a good source of gossip in either of those locations, you realize," Athos said.

Svetlana nodded again. They had no information at all on what the ghosts might be doing, nor any way to obtain it. They still had one friend within the Air Fleet, Svetlana's ex-girlfriend Narcissa Marsh, who had been particularly helpful in getting the crew of *The Silent Monsoon* access to the Air Fleet's copy of the map that would lead to the Last Emperor's Hoard. Svetlana was forever grateful that she and Narci had managed to patch things up after their breakup a decade and a half ago and remained mostly amicable in recent months. "We can at least see if Narci has any information for us," she suggested.

~

Though *The Silent Monsoon* was docked at Rrusadon, Svetlana had found a number of tasks around the ship to keep herself busy. She knew that eventually she'd need to go visit Lar, but she wasn't ready to have the inevitable conversation about his "bride gift."

She'd sent Athos out to send an airwave message to Chickie, known both by his nickname and as Lord Algernon Boughorpington the Third, a member of the nobility who had become a friend to the crew of *The Silent Monsoon* after Svetlana attended a party on his airship. He lived on Heliopolis, the former home port of *The Silent Monsoon*, which gave him access to the Air Fleet Headquarters and a number of their former associates with whom they could no longer correspond directly. His high station allowed him to maintain a wide array of friendships, including one with Narci. Since all the crew members were currently wanted by the Air Fleet for various and sundry crimes, passing messages through a member of the nobility to their one remaining contact within the Air Fleet who didn't want them arrested was the best they could do.

Until Athos returned, though, Svetlana had reached a point where she couldn't really invent any more tasks that needed doing before she could go see Lar. Everything on the airship was tidy and well ordered.

As her gaze fell upon the cloud-generator on the bridge, she bristled again. Perhaps it would be best if she went for a walk to clear her head before she went to visit Lar.

"Captain?" Indigo's voice lilted out from the bridge's open windows.

"Saved by Indy," Svetlana muttered, then stepped onto the bridge. "Yes?"

"What's this button do?" Indigo was crouched down near the base of the cloud generator, pointing at a round copper button without a label. The top of the device had plenty of indicators of which buttons did what, but this strange unlabeled button was an oddity.

"Are you sure it's a button?" Svetlana asked.

"Haven't pressed it."

"Probably shouldn't, eh?"

Indigo shrugged his slight shoulders. "Or we could and see what happens."

"Or you could ask Martin the next time he comes by, instead."

"Okay. Or you could ask Lar?"

"I could," Svetlana said, trying to keep her expression neutral.

Indigo remained on the floor, his gaze now transfixed on the button, as though staring at it for long enough would cause it to reveal its secrets to him.

Svetlana shook her head, searching for a good way to distract Indigo from his current fixation. "How's Drassilis?"

Drassilis was an automaton constructed by Lady Elinor de Whittvy. After Drassilis had been severely damaged just prior to Lady de Whittvy's death, Svetlana had brought him back to *The Silent Monsoon* for Indigo to repair so they could unlock any of Lady de Whittvy's secrets the automaton possessed. Now that he was fully rebuilt, he had become an honorary member of the crew and a fast friend of Indigo's.

"Fine."

Svetlana chuckled softly. "Okay, where's Drassilis?"

"Engine room."

"Are you going to sit and stare at that button until you know what it does?"

"Yes."

"Alright, then I'll go talk to Lar," Svetlana said, straightening her jacket. "If you get hungry, you'll go eat, right?"

Indigo shrugged. "Can you hurry?"

"Yes, I'll hurry." *So much for clearing my head first.*

~

Svetlana had grown accustomed to the humidity and heat on Rrusadon, so normally she walked slowly and enjoyed the lush greenness of plant life that was lacking in her normal day-to-day life. But the cloud generator, both what it did and what it meant, weighed heavily enough on her mind that she found herself walking quickly and with purpose, rather than enjoying a leisurely stroll.

She bypassed the public entrance to Lar's house and entered instead through a side entrance he had encouraged her to use, since she was welcome to visit any time. A twinge of guilt ran through her as she did so, mostly because her thoughts ran toward being furious with Lar. It wasn't enough to stop her from accepting the convenience of not having to wait to see the mayor.

Once inside, she made her way through the opulently decorated house, passing by many fountains adorned with gilded statues. The fountains at least served a purpose here, keeping the temperature inside the house considerably cooler than the weather, but their grandeur was a trace of the Kavisoli ostentatiousness that Lar didn't exhibit in his personal life. His private portions of the house were simple and utilitarian, which Svetlana appreciated. It made the gift of the cloud generator all the more baffling to her, too. He knew she didn't like lavish gifts, and she had made it clear that she loved her ship just the way it was, turning down his offer to have it replaced or retrofitted. So lost she was in her own thoughts, Svetlana entered Lar's study unannounced.

She wasn't the only one there—two elderly women and an older man, perhaps in his fifties, sat on a padded bench that wasn't normally a part of the study décor, conversing with Lar.

The women looked similar enough to be sisters, with their thick, dark hair twisted into elaborate loops of braid and curl, and their dark skin absorbing the scant light in the study. Both dressed in flowing gray dresses that bore no resemblance to the fashions in the large cities but looked far more elegant and comfortable than most fashion.

The man's skin was a pale bronze, or at least that was the color it appeared to have through the wreath of fragrant tobacco smoke that emanated from his cigar. He waved the haze away with a hand laden with gold rings and smiled at Svetlana. His bald head shone nearly as brightly as his jewelry and brilliant white teeth.

Lar looked up at Svetlana, his gray eyes sparkling. "And here's my girl now."

Svetlana's back stiffened, and her mouth tightened. She wasn't going to start yelling with these other people in the room, but Lar calling her "my girl" was hard to swallow.

Lar seemed to read Svetlana's expression. His smile faded, and he offered his audience an open-handed conciliatory gesture. "I'm sorry, my friends. This may not be the best time for me to make introductions. Sveta and I have things to discuss first, and then I'm sure she'll be pleased to get to know you all better."

Svetlana stood to one side of the door and tried to give each of the departing people a polite nod. But the smile she pasted on to do so made her face ache, and she dropped it the moment the last person had passed her. Closing the door behind them, she paused with her back to Lar.

"Sveta, is something wrong?"

"I didn't ask for a gift." Her voice was low and measured, but she could hear the quaver in it as she spoke.

Lar chuckled. "That's why it's a gift, my love. It was meant to be a surprise."

Turning to face Lar, Svetlana said, "That's not the sort of surprise I needed today."

"Did it not help you rescue Jo?"

"It did. It's just the nature of the giving."

His brow knit. "I don't understand."

"I think you do, and you're just playing dumb. I'm not the sort of woman who is wooed by—" She trailed off, frustration taking her words before she could articulate them. "And Martin."

"What about Martin? Who has he been attempting to woo?"

Svetlana sighed. "No one. He needs to learn to watch his tongue."

"Was he disrespectful to someone on your crew?"

"No, no, it's not that, it's—"

Lar cut her off. "I was under the impression that he was someone you appreciated having around. That's why I sent him."

Svetlana shook her head. "That's what I hate about the idle rich. They just send their people and their toys to try to fix everything."

Lar's expression shifted, his jaw now clenched and his eyes going cold. "You think I'm idle?"

Svetlana threw her hands up and gestured to the study around them, where Lar spent the majority of his time when he wasn't swimming laps in the pool or dining and drinking with visitors. It was simply decorated, compared to the rest of the house, but most people Svetlana knew did not have the space to maintain an entire wing of private rooms that included a study and large bedroom. "I don't know what else to call it."

"I see." His tone had taken on the same iciness as his expression. "So I should stop sending you gifts and crew and do things myself, is that it?"

"I don't know," Svetlana said, her exasperation rising. "I just think ... Things have gotten too ..." She shook her head, unable to complete any of her thoughts. Even while furious at Lar, she still longed to be in his arms, not fighting with him. If her pride hadn't been so fierce, perhaps they wouldn't be fighting. But she'd started it. Now she just needed to be done with it. "I shouldn't have come by. I'll ... I'll see you later, I guess."

"Very well," Lar said. "You know your way out."

Svetlana gave him a curt nod and showed herself out of the house.

~

Svetlana fumed as she headed back to her ship. The conversation hadn't gotten them anywhere other than angry—or angrier, in her case—with each other. She hadn't asked him about the meaning of his gift, and she'd forgotten to find out what the strange unmarked button did. And he'd been wounded by her calling him idle. She wasn't sure what else you would call someone who had few actual responsibilities. As best as she could tell, Mayor was an honorary title, and the Kavisoli family did all of the heavy lifting for keeping Rrusadon running smoothly, while Lar just smiled and charmed visitors. She'd told herself countless times that she wasn't jealous when he had to entertain people other than her, but that emotion was beginning to creep into her thoughts.

When she arrived back on *The Silent Monsoon*, Indigo was still crouched beside the cloud generator. He looked up at her expectantly.

"Sorry, Indy. I didn't find anything out. I've half a mind to chuck that thing overboard."

Indigo's eyes widened, and he rose to wrap his arms around the device as though he was hugging it. "No, Captain, we need it."

"I know. That's why I haven't yet. We'll just have to see what it can do after we've left."

"Are we leaving soon?"

Svetlana looked toward the gangplank, which Athos was currently striding up. "I need to talk to Athos first."

Athos stepped onto the bridge, and his brow furrowed as he spotted Indigo, half his rail-thin frame draped across the cloud generator. "What's he—"

"Don't ask," Svetlana said with a wave of her hand. "What's the news?"

"Eh, bad to worse," Athos replied. "The Air Fleet is preparing for an expedition to resettle Barkovia."

Svetlana narrowed her good eye. Barkovia was the location of her last battle as a member of the Air Fleet. The Republic had declared the small island's inhabitants in a state of rebellion, and troops ostensibly under her command had helped wipe out the population, earning her the nickname "The Butcher of Barkovia." She'd resigned her commission immediately afterward, but the nickname had followed her, and she still didn't like hearing the name of that island. "What for? There's nothing there."

"No *one*, but that doesn't mean *nothing*," Athos said. "Likely they're going to extract some sort of resource."

"Or they need a launching point that's nearer to the treasure than any other Republic states," Svetlana said. "And where better to set that up than an island whose inhabitants you wiped out half a dozen years ago?"

"Like I said, bad news."

"What's the worse?"

Athos cast his gaze skyward. "Ghost ship sighting."

Indigo gasped. "Where?"

"Near Windsor," Athos said, "and heading west."

Indigo frowned, then scrambled to the map. He found the platform city of Windsor and looked up at Svetlana. "Captain!"

"Near Dougou, yep," Svetlana said, naming the village where Indigo had been born and raised, at least until the crew of *The Silent Monsoon* had crash-landed near there a few years back, and took the boy on as their mechanic.

"Can we go?" Indigo asked.

Svetlana nodded slowly. Though running off to a location that was hard to reach by airwave would make getting information from their friends difficult, Windsor was a short flight from the island where Dougou lay, so they wouldn't be completely out of touch. Svetlana and Athos could fly the *Monsoon* together, with Jo still laid up by her injury. They could find out what the ghosts had done in Windsor and plan the *Monsoon*'s next steps in a place where Svetlana could get some distance from Lar.

CHAPTER THREE

Rrusadon was often humid, but Dougou gave new meaning to the word. Nearer to the coast than most island settlements, it suffered from a combination of steamy ocean breezes and the dense jungle that sat just inland of its location. Scoured white sands surrounded the village, dotted with their own plant life sprouting up in any place where the boiling tides rarely reached.

The village itself comprised a variety of small structures in many building styles and materials, possibly salvaged from previously existing buildings or ships. Some used organic pieces as well, large fronds from some of the jungle foliage that ranged from fresh and green to a more weathered yellowish-brown.

When Svetlana and her crew debarked *The Silent Monsoon*, Indigo was the only one who had dressed for the occasion, shucking his shirt and wearing only short trousers. He rarely wore shoes on board the ship, and Svetlana was not surprised to see that he hadn't bothered with them here, either.

"First order of business? New clothes," Athos said, squinting in the bright sun as he surveyed the landscape.

A crowd of villagers had assembled nearby, staring at the airship and crew. Few of them wore clothes more substantial than short trousers or dresses, some with shirts as well, all loose and billowy. They spoke in hushed voices, but one or two of the younger people who had assembled pointed at Indigo as they chattered. Here, Indigo's blue hair didn't look out of place, as nearly every head in the village was adorned with hair in any of a dozen different bright colors. His paleness, however, was an oddity that he shared with few of the villagers, most of whom ranged across a vibrant spectrum of shades of brown.

"Indy, is Deliah from Dougou?" Annette asked.

29

Indigo cocked his head to the side and shook it, but then he followed Annette's gaze toward the crowd. He gasped and ran down the gangplank, leaping the gap between its end and the ground.

By the time the rest of the crew reached him, most of the villagers had dispersed, and Indigo had enveloped Deliah in a hug, covering most of her face with his wavy blue hair.

"Hello, Captain," Deliah said, her voice muffled.

Svetlana studied the girl. Deliah was a friend of Indigo's from Heliopolis, who had travelled on *The Silent Monsoon* occasionally in recent months. They hadn't seen her since she'd fled the ship after kissing Indigo a couple of months previous, leaving the crew to worry about where she'd wandered off to and who she might be sharing their secrets with.

Deliah seemed to be no worse for the wear since her most recent departure from *The Silent Monsoon*. She was dressed similarly to the inhabitants of Dougou, rather than the ragtag assortment of layers she normally wore, but her bright orangish-yellow pigtails still stuck out from the sides of her head at their customary uneven angles.

"Good to see you, Deliah," Svetlana said. "Is everything alright?"

Deliah nodded, extricating herself from Indigo's grasp. "I'm alright. Not everything."

"How do you mean?" Athos asked.

Deliah gave him a quick glance, but then turned to Svetlana to answer Athos's question. "The ghosts are going to Bonebriar."

Svetlana's shoulders slumped as Deliah's answer confirmed her worst fear. "So you were with the ghosts?"

Deliah nodded, gaze cast toward the ground as she drew circles in the sand with her bare toes.

"What do the ghosts know?" Svetlana asked.

Deliah didn't respond but instead took Indigo's hand and began to pull him toward one of the small houses nearby. "Indy's mother lives here."

"Deliah, wait," Svetlana said. "Did you take the information we had to the ghosts?"

"I don't want to talk about it," Deliah said, setting her mouth in a firm line.

30

"We're not angry with you, Deliah." Svetlana tried to keep her expression as even as possible. She had suspected the girl was taking their information to someone when she left *The Silent Monsoon* so suddenly—especially having just distracted Indigo with a kiss—but at this point, Svetlana was more concerned than angry about it. It was inevitable that all the groups pursuing the Last Emperor's Hoard were getting close to their quarry. Finally, Svetlana said, "We just want to know how much they know."

"They know where to look." Deliah shrugged. "They'll go soon."

"How soon?" Annette asked.

"Maybe now. Maybe too late for you."

Svetlana gave Deliah a terse nod. "Alright, thank you. Take Indy to see his mother. We'll be along shortly."

As the teenagers ran off toward the village, Athos stepped between them and Svetlana. "So everybody knows, huh?"

"I'm not surprised," Svetlana said. "We knew the Air Fleet was getting close, so we tried to slow them down. I don't know if there is any slowing down ghosts, but I'd love to find out."

"That's not the sort of thing I have books on, unfortunately," Annette said, "and I truly don't know anyone who would, either."

"It's not a commonly pursued course of study," Svetlana said. "Bullets don't hurt them, blades do. I don't think we can launch blades from the cannon."

"Not in any useful way," Athos said. "Any idea I can come up with based on that would just wind up making our ship look like a bristly-back, and I don't really think we want to fly near enough to ram a ghost ship."

"Not without Jo on the wheel, at least," Svetlana said. "With her out of commission, we may not be able to do much about the ghosts getting closer to the Hoard." She sighed, the exhaustion of their jail break and her fight with Lar finally catching up to her. Though the need to pursue the Gem of the Seas was pressing, she also had no good ideas on how to do so. "It's been a long few days. Let's get some new clothes for everyone and relax a bit, and then we'll see what we think of things, eh?"

~

Finally dressed in the local fashion and out of the harsh direct sunlight, Svetlana understood how people could stand to live in such a climate. The light wind making its way into the village smelled of the sulfurous ocean, but it brought with it some cooler air. The thin fabric of the clothing allowed the breeze to go straight through it. Most of the locals stuck to the shaded areas as much as they could, limiting their exposure to the scorching sun.

"This is some heat for autumn," Svetlana observed as she and Annette sat beneath a large palm frond umbrella, enjoying a cool, fruity tea very unlike the strong black tea they had gotten here previously.

"This part of the world is always warm," Annette replied.

"Even before the Boiling?" Svetlana asked. She'd never been big on history, but Annette was an enthusiastic student of the subject.

Annette shrugged. "Maybe not as warm as it is now, but it's why there are still so many vacation spots near this latitude. Warm sun and sandy beaches."

"I've never understood the appeal of any of the places you call vacation spots, Doc."

"That's because you don't know how to enjoy relaxation, Captain," Annette fired back with a lazy grin.

Athos and Jo strolled up to join the captain and doctor. Of the women on the ship, only Jo had opted for a short, loose fitting dress. Svetlana and Annette had both selected loose blouses and short trousers, while Athos wore only a light vest with his short trousers.

All of them had left their boots on the ship, but they'd found the ground here a little less forgiving than they'd hoped, and selected local footwear as well, which, as best as Svetlana could tell, consisted of something like fabric-wrapped twine holding pieces of bark to the soles of their feet. It had taken a little bit of getting used to, and Svetlana still wasn't sure how to deal with the grains of sand that inevitably clung to one's feet while walking in these shoes.

"Indy and Deliah still visiting with Indy's mum?" Athos asked as he and Jo ducked under the edge of the umbrella. Though his copper skin nearly glowed in the light of the setting sun, sweat beaded his face.

Svetlana nodded. "Feeling any better, Jo?"

Jo shrugged but gave a half nod. She gestured toward Svetlana's legs as though she were brushing them away and moved to sit on part of the bench Svetlana occupied.

Swinging her legs to the side, Svetlana made room for Jo, turning so she faced Annette's bench.

Annette did the same for Athos, after he helped himself to a glass of tea. "Any news in the village?" she asked

"I've heard plenty of local rumors, but these folks don't get out much, nor do they have many visitors," Athos said. "They seem to have never seen anything like the ghost ship before, but no one seems particularly surprised that such a thing exists. Our ship, and Indy, are much more interesting to them. It's all more excitement than they've had in a while."

Jo pulled out her notebook and scribbled a note, then passed it to Svetlana.

"'Do you believe Deliah that it's too late to find the Hoard?'" Svetlana read. "It's not too late till we know someone else has the treasure."

Jo gestured for Svetlana to return her notebook, and wrote another quick note, which she showed to the others as well. "Then why are we still here?"

"We only just got here," Athos said, "and you're still in no shape for flying."

Jo shrugged.

"He's not wrong, Jo," Annette said gently. "You have to give yourself time to heal. If we go off galivanting around too soon, you're likely to hurt yourself more."

"Got a question for you, Jo," Svetlana said, pulling the piece of paper she had torn from Jo's notebook from the pocket of her trousers and unfolding it. She pointed at the two incomplete lines. "Athos and Indy figured out most of this. But we can't quite place the second part. Is it something you've heard before?"

Jo shook her head, then wrote in the notebook and held it up. "None of the other staves filled in the blanks?"

"Nothing conclusive." Annette retrieved a sheet of paper from her pocket and laid the sketch of the map that purportedly led to the Last Emperor's Hoard beside Jo's notes. She pointed at the portion of the map where the crew believed the text belonged. "We've got something that might be a word ending with 'less' in the top line, and probably 'of pool' or 'of pools' in the bottom line.

Or some other word starting with 'poo.'" She smirked. "We're pretty sure it's not 'poo.'"

Jo took the paper from Svetlana and held her pen above the lower lines, then started moving it to the right, pausing and looking up at Annette, her head cocked to the side.

"How far out?" Annette asked.

Jo nodded.

"No idea," Annette said. "We don't know where the phrases started on the map."

"Let's assume there's not much in between," Svetlana said, looking at the phrases again. "'Were the Oceans to cease ... less.' Could be ceaseless, but that doesn't make sense. 'Geysers would turn to ... of pools.'" She shook her head. "There are definitely words we're missing."

"'Were the Oceans to cease' ... well, boiling, one might presume," Athos suggested.

"But that doesn't go with 'less,'" Annette reminded him. "'Were the Oceans to cease boiling less'?"

"Doesn't seem too poetic," Svetlana said. "Okay, the other part. 'Geysers would turn to ... of pools.' What 'of pools'? What other words end with 'of'?"

"Proof?" Athos suggested. "Roof? Aloof?"

Svetlana shook her head. "Accurate, but they don't make sense either." She placed her finger over the word "of" and focused on the other words around it. "Geysers would turn to pools," she muttered.

As the pieces connected, Svetlana felt as if she had been punched in the chest, with all the air escaping her lungs in a rush. When she regained her breath, she gasped, "Sweet Skyfather. If the geysers turned into pools, where does that leave the platform cities?"

Around her, Annette's, Athos's, and Jo's eyes all went wide.

"Doom," Jo whispered.

Svetlana nodded slowly. "I knew I didn't trust the Air Fleet with the Gem. Now I know why."

Annette held up her hands in front of her. "The Air Fleet has prospered from the platform cities. Do you really think they'd be so quick to let them fall?"

"They may not have thought this all the way through," Svetlana said. "This might be worth getting a message to Bobby."

She regretted the words as soon as she'd said them. Rear Admiral Robert Beauregard, Bobby only to his closest friends, had been Svetlana's mentor in the Air Fleet. They had maintained their friendship even after she left the Fleet and became an independent shipping contractor, but he had made it clear at Bonebriar that he was more loyal to the Air Fleet and the High Council than to his friends, and Svetlana had written him off as a loss. The fact that she and her crew were wanted by the Air Fleet was the secondary reason contacting Bobby was a bad idea, but the first reason was far worse in her mind.

Athos was already shaking his head. "Bad idea, Sveta."

"Yeah, I know. Knee-jerk reaction." She chewed at her lip. "Jo, did you see or hear anything at all when you were at Republican City, or Aldfort, or anywhere along the way, that might tell us if the High Council already has this information?"

Jo's eyebrows knit together in concentration.

As Jo considered Svetlana's question, Annette spoke up. "Do you think Chickie has any contacts among the High Council? Or someone he could ask?"

"I doubt it," Svetlana said. "If he'd known a good way to get us information from the High Council's chambers, I think he'd have brought it up already, and then we wouldn't be seeing what Jo remembers."

Jo had picked up her pencil and scribbled a few words, but then she crossed them out. She let out an exasperated sigh, wrote something else, and handed the notebook to Svetlana.

"She crossed out something about Republican City and Heliopolis, and then wrote, 'Why would they care about the platforms? They have the Fleet'," Svetlana said, frowning.

"How many airships would it take to hold up a platform city like Republican City or Heliopolis?" Annette asked. "Is that even possible?"

Svetlana nodded. "Theoretically speaking, yes. The engines used on the platform cities aren't that different from the engines on airships. And back when the platform cities were put into place, that's how they moved them over the geysers—with airships."

"So it's not impossible to do the opposite," Athos said. "You're a genius, Jo Dean. The High Council isn't going to care, because they've got the resources to save the two places they care about.

They'll pull the Air Fleet and the nobles out of every other platform city and then let them all fall."

"I'd be shocked if they pulled all the nobles," Svetlana said. "They'll probably just save the ones who didn't buy their way in, or the few who live on a platform city who are willing to sacrifice thousands of people if it means they get to keep their money and titles."

Annette's normally warm brown skin had gone ashen. "You can't be serious. It's hundreds of thousands of people who would die if the platform cities fell."

Svetlana nodded. "Hundreds of thousands of people the High Council considers expendable. There's always a contingent of noble families who talks about things being the way they were in the old days, before people bought their way into the Senate, when it was just the 'true' nobility."

"I should send an airwave to my—" Athos began, then cut himself off with a bitter chuckle. "Oh, who am I kidding. There aren't enough airwaves in the world to get the news to everyone I know who will die because of this."

Svetlana shook her head. "No. We're not going to let them die. We've got to find the Gem first. It's the only option."

"And then what?" Annette asked.

"I'll figure that out when we get there," Svetlana said.

CHAPTER FOUR

The crew of *The Silent Monsoon*, plus their honorary members, Deliah and Drassilis, gathered in the mess. Dust motes danced through the air, illuminated by the filtered sunlight streaming in through the high windows and highlighted the maps, notes, and other assorted scraps of paper that covered the broad oak table. Drassilis's metallic body, larger than that of a human but still modelled after an adult male, gleamed in the light. Only when someone examined his lower half more closely would they realize that his resemblance to a human ended at his waist, his lower body being cylindrical and wheeled. The sunlight also created ominous looking shadows within the filigree mask that served as his face. His over-large eyes moved across the assembled information while Annette tilted her head from side to side and rearranged a few pieces.

Svetlana climbed onto one of the chairs, perching on the back with her feet on the seat, her customary position for crew meetings. "We think we've got a pretty good idea of where to look for the Last Emperor's Hoard, and we need to make sure that we're the first ones to get there so no one else has a chance to get their hands on it."

"Ghost ship might already be there," Deliah piped up.

"Yep, that's a possibility," Svetlana agreed. "But we have no good way of finding that out."

Deliah nodded. "Yes. I do."

"What do you mean?" Athos asked.

"Aetherwave," Deliah said.

"Like an airwave?" Svetlana asked, her shoulders tensing.

Deliah nodded, her mouth a firm line. "Works best on platforms."

"Does that mean you can call the ghosts, across any distance?" Athos asked.

"Mostly," Deliah said. "Doesn't work here."

Jo murmured, "Bluesummer?"

Deliah blushed crimson and nodded. "Yes. I'm sorry."

Svetlana glanced at Athos, Jo, and Annette in turn, then jerked her chin in the direction of the hallway. As they all moved toward the door of the mess, she said, "Indy, you and Deliah and Drassilis stay here a minute, okay?"

"We're not leaving her behind," Indigo said, his voice forceful.

"Nobody suggested that, Indy," Annette said. "We're just taking stock of all the information we have right now." As Annette joined the others in the hallway, she lowered her voice. "We're not suggesting that, are we?"

Svetlana shook her head. "My question is whether or not what she's suggesting is even possible."

Jo shrugged.

"We don't know what Aetherwhere can and can't do. I mean, if you'd asked me six months ago about Aetherwhere, I would have just laughed it off. Now?" Athos shrugged. "Anything's possible."

"Let's say it is possible," Svetlana said. "It means she can find out where the ghost ship is, which is useful."

"But does it mean they can find us too?" Annette asked.

"I'd have to assume as much," Athos said, rubbing at his chin. "There are communication systems that work in only a single direction, but whatever this Aetherwave is, the ghosts know about it. They wouldn't set up Deliah to be able to hear them if they can't hear her too."

"We'll have to be careful what we let Deliah know, then," Svetlana suggested.

"As much as we can," Annette said, glancing back into the mess. "She already knows plenty. Unless you want to cut off Indy and Drassilis too, she'll find out more."

Svetlana chewed at her lip. Annette was right. And while it might be dangerous to let the ghosts know where *The Silent Monsoon* was headed, it seemed too late to stop them, if they had a direct line into Deliah's mind. "I don't want to go around telling everyone where we're at, but if there's nothing to be done about it that doesn't involve dropping Deliah off somewhere, then we'll just have to make the best of it. She might not be earning shares yet, but I think she's part of the crew at this point."

Athos chuckled. "I'd suspect so, at least for as long as Indy's flying with us."

Svetlana nodded. "All agreed?"

Athos and Annette both nodded, followed by Jo a moment later.

After the crew all gave their assent, Svetlana stepped back into the mess and resumed her perch on the back of the chair as the others returned to their seats. "Deliah, is it true you can contact the ghosts and find out where they are, and they can find you too?"

"Sometimes," Deliah said.

"Then if they call you, let us know, okay?"

Deliah nodded.

"Next order of business is how we're going to access a treasure that's lost underwater, right?" Athos asked.

Svetlana nodded. "Indy, you have any ideas on that?"

Indigo's brow knit, and he twisted a lock of hair around his finger as he thought. Finally, he said, "Diving bell."

"What's that?" Athos asked.

"Pressurized tiny ship that goes underwater. Some people here live in them."

"Underwater?" Svetlana asked.

"No, on land. But they could go underwater, if they lock the door."

"I've heard old stories about underwater exploration, but—" Annette trailed off. "These days, that would be suicide. Unless you could insulate the diving bell."

Indigo nodded. "Find the big one and put a smaller one inside. Convert heating coils to cooling coils."

Drassilis chirped as though he was clearing his throat, and then said, "What young Indigo proposes could be done. I am familiar with the conversion of heating coils to cooling coils, and vice versa. I can assist him in this endeavor."

Annette nodded slowly. "That could work, I think, though we'd need some sort of device to pick up the treasure outside of the diving bell. Like a net, maybe?"

Jo held up her notebook, showing the crew what she'd written there. "Net out of rigging lines. Heavy but sturdy."

Svetlana nodded as she considered the idea Indigo had laid out. "Can we get everything you would need here?"

Indigo shook his head. "Only the diving bells."

"If we can get you the other pieces, how long do you think this will take?"

"A week. Maybe two."

"Any way to speed it up?" Svetlana asked

"Captain Tereshchenko," Drassilis said, "I require minimal sleep and sustenance. If the pieces can be obtained quickly, I calculate that we can reduce the time it may take us to construct this enhanced diving bell. If the work would take Indigo alone two weeks, with my assistance, we may be able to complete the work in just over five days."

"Thank you, Drassilis," Svetlana said. "That's a better estimate for our timeline. But we want to ensure it works, too, so we'll need some time for tests."

"Understood, Captain Tereshchenko. Perhaps one full week, then."

"Jo, do you feel up for a short flight, with me?" Svetlana asked.

Jo nodded, one corner of her mouth turning up slightly. Her eyes belied a glimmer of pain, but they went back to their normal appearance as soon as she stopped trying to smile.

"Indy, I want you, Drassilis, and Doc to work on this diving bell plan. You'll need to make us a shopping list of things we can find on Windsor. Jo, Athos, Deliah, and I will head up to the platform. Athos can do the shopping, Deliah can see if she can find the ghosts, and I'm going to try to reach Narci."

Athos frowned. "Narci? What for now?"

Though Svetlana wouldn't admit it aloud, part of her motivation was to make sure her ex-lover was alright. But she couched her response in terms of the plans the crew was concocting. "See if she's heard anything more at Air Fleet, about preparations to float Heliopolis or Republican City somewhere safer. That's going to be an enormous operation. If she hasn't heard anything about it, then maybe we're not in as big of a rush as we thought."

"Maybe," Athos agreed, "but I don't think this is the sort of thing we want to delay too long, Sveta."

"I'm well aware," Svetlana replied, "but we've got to go to Windsor anyway, so we might as well keep ourselves as informed as we can."

Jo held up her notebook again. "What do I do in Windsor?"

"Rest," Annette said. "Doctor's orders."

Jo saluted Annette.

"This sounds like we've got ourselves a plan," Svetlana said.

~

Chimneys on Windsor belched smoke in varying shades of gray and brown, all the way to something almost as black as the sea at night. Svetlana sniffed at the air as she and Jo brought *The Silent Monsoon* into its docking slip. "Jo, can we all borrow some of your scarves? This air doesn't look good to breathe."

Jo nodded.

Svetlana maneuvered the ship onto the docking struts and locked the controls. As soon as *The Silent Monsoon* was stationary, Jo hurried down the back stairs.

Athos surfaced a moment later, with Deliah behind him. Both of them looked at the sky and frowned.

"People live here?" Deliah asked.

"Jo's bringing us scarves to keep some of that bad air out of our noses and mouths. I hope it'll help," Svetlana replied. "Shopping list?" she asked Athos.

He nodded. "Some of it's a little bit specialized. I'm going to see if I can't hire an assistant to make sure I get what I'm asking for, and so I get a good deal."

Jo returned to the bridge, carrying three filmy scarves in brilliant jewel tones. She beckoned Athos with a crook of her finger and set to winding the scarf around his lower face. Though the fabric looked very thin, when Jo was done with the scarf, Athos was nearly unrecognizable.

He was also muffled when he spoke. "Say hi to Narci for me," he said to Svetlana, then gave Jo's shoulder a gentle squeeze, and set out to lower the gangplank.

Jo wrapped a scarf around Deliah's face next, a deep blue that contrasted sharply with Deliah's orange-yellow hair. Deliah hummed the entire time while Jo worked and squealed in muted delight when the scarf nearly blocked her humming.

"Wait for me, Deliah," Svetlana said as the girl began to move toward the deck.

"Aye, Captain."

When Svetlana turned back to face Jo, the pilot had already twisted and turned the scarf into something that looked more like a loose helmet. Jo gently slipped it over the top of Svetlana's head. The fabric covered the lower parts of Svetlana's face with some thickness, but as Jo picked at it lightly, a thin, gauzy layer fell across Svetlana's eyes. She could still see through the scarf, but it concealed her eyes from view.

Jo winked at Svetlana, and then raised her eyebrows as though she were asking a question.

"Genius, Jo Dean," Svetlana replied. "We shouldn't be long, unless Deliah's Aetherwave takes longer than airwaves."

Deliah did not answer but picked gingerly at the fabric of her scarf as though she were trying to bring the back of it up to cover her hair and eyes like Svetlana's.

Jo looked at Deliah, then held her arms out straight to either side with her hands marking out a measure of her full armspan. She cocked her head slightly toward Svetlana, then moved her hands closer together, showing a shorter measure, and nodded at Deliah.

"Too short," Deliah said.

Jo nodded.

With a chuckle, Svetlana slung an arm around Deliah's slight shoulders. "Good guess, Deliah. Much as you and Jo might have fun all day with this, we need to find out what we can. Ship's yours, Jo."

Svetlana and Deliah made their way down the gangplank, and Svetlana scanned the streets for signs pointing out the airwave office. Deliah slipped her hand into Svetlana's and pulled her toward one of the streets radiating from the docks.

"Where are you taking me?" Svetlana asked.

"Airwave first," Deliah replied.

As they neared the end of the street, Svetlana identified the sign Deliah had seen, which had been obscured by the portion of the scarf that held the layer of fabric concealing her eyes. She considered lifting her veil to allow her to see better but thought twice about that idea when she and Deliah passed a pair of Air Fleet privates.

Deliah led Svetlana to a door, and moved to push it open, but Svetlana tugged at Deliah's hand before the girl could touch the door. "This is an Air Fleet office," Svetlana murmured. "Did you see any signs for other airwave offices?"

"Only one on the signs," Deliah said.

"Alright, then you wait out here. I have an idea."

Deliah nodded and released Svetlana's hand.

Svetlana's hand trembled as she pushed open the door, her mind awhirl with possible ways to get a message to Narci without revealing her identity. She hunched her shoulders slightly as she walked in, making herself look stooped.

The private manning the airwave equipment, a young dark-skinned woman with her hair swept up in a navy-blue scarf that matched her Air Fleet uniform, looked up at Svetlana's approach. The young woman's brow furrowed as she took in Svetlana's strange appearance, between the loose scarf and heavy wool jacket. "Can I help you, ma'am?"

"I need to send a message," Svetlana said, intentionally making her voice sound creaky, like an elderly person.

"This station is only for Air Fleet messages, ma'am."

"Oh, my apologies. I need to send a message to my cousin's daughter. She's with the Air Fleet. Where would I find another airwave station?"

The young woman hesitated, then said, "Well, if you need to get a message to an Air Fleet member, I can help you. What is your cousin's daughter's name?"

"Narcissa Marsh," Svetlana said. "I believe she's a high rank of some sort."

"As you say, ma'am. Where is she stationed?"

"Heliopolis."

"Very good, and the message? Could you write it down for me?"

Svetlana shook her head. "Oh, no. I'm afraid my eyesight isn't what it used to be. Just send her a message to contact Uncle Algie as soon as she can."

"Algie?" the young woman asked.

"Short for Algernon, my dear. A-L-G-I-E."

"Very good, ma'am. Will you await her response here?"

"Oh, no, dearie. I have shopping to do. I'll come back later to see if there's a reply."

The airwave operated nodded. "And your name, ma'am? In case I'm off shift when you return?"

"Leave it to the attention of Beatrice," Svetlana said, borrowing the name of her grandmother. "If you don't mind, I would like directions to the other airwave station, in case I have a mind to send more messages today."

"Of course, ma'am," the private replied as she jotted down her notes for the airwave.

~

Back outside of the airwave office, Svetlana found Deliah sprawled on the cobblestone street, half-sitting against a nearby building. The girl's eyes were closed, but her eyeballs darted back and forth beneath her eyelids.

Svetlana lay a gentle hand on Deliah's shoulder, and the girl lurched forward, eyes flying open.

"Are you alright?" Svetlana asked.

Deliah nodded. "Aetherwave."

Taking a step backward, Svetlana looked into Deliah's eyes, which focused immediately on the captain's face. "You're not talking to them right now, are you?"

"No, I was before. What did you want to know?"

Svetlana hesitated, chewing at the inside of her lip. They needed to know where the ghosts were, but she suspected that the ghosts would not answer such a query, even if it came from one of their former associates. "I want to meet with them. They can choose the time and location."

Deliah's brow furrowed, but she nodded and closed her eyes again. In an instant, her eyeballs began their erratic dance beneath her eyelids, and less than a minute passed before she opened her eyes again. "They have your message."

"No response?" Svetlana asked.

"Not yet. The message is in the Aetherwhere. They'll respond when they want to."

Svetlana chuckled. "It is like airwaves, then. I got directions to another airwave office. Let's head over there and contact Chickie."

~

By the time Svetlana and Deliah reached the other airwave office, the filthy air in Windsor was affecting both of them, even with Jo's cleverly wrapped scarves. Deliah coughed nearly constantly, and Svetlana found it harder to draw breath than it was even at high altitudes in an airship.

Inside the office, breathing was not much easier, especially with the crowd of people inside. Svetlana scanned the room, then said, "You can wait outside if you prefer, Deliah. Hopefully this won't take long."

"Rather stay here." Loud barking coughs punctuated either side of Deliah's words.

Svetlana pushed her way through the crowd toward the airwave operator, pulling a Quinpence from her pocket as she did. It was far more than she ought to pay for messages, but she wanted the operator's attention and to be able to transact her business quickly.

The fair-haired, ruddy-skinned, young man spotted the flash of gold and was waiting for Svetlana when she approached the counter, flashing a brilliant smile, though his gaze was focused on the coin instead of Svetlana's face.

"Two messages, and possible follow-up responses?" she asked.

"That will suffice," he said, handing her two slips of paper.

Composing the message to Chickie was easy. "Looking for our mutual friend. Have you seen her? -ST" Though they had many mutual friends, the term was their agreed upon shorthand for Narci without mentioning her by name.

For the message to Narci, Svetlana had to consider more carefully what she wrote, since that message would be transmitted to the Air Fleet Headquarters, which was sure to be monitoring any communications that came in for Rear Admiral Marsh, especially after recent events. Narci had warned Svetlana that her assistance with getting Svetlana and some of her crew into the Aetherwhere Division at Air Fleet Headquarters would likely cause future problems for Narci, but she'd also agreed to go along with their plans, since she, too, doubted the Air Fleet was working toward a noble goal in this situation.

In the end, she simply wrote, "Status update?" She signed it with the name "C. Marsh," hoping a note from a plausible relative of Narci's would slip through unnoticed.

The operator took the two slips and busied himself with entering them immediately, then moved on to another portion of the machine where he began scribbling out responses.

Svetlana was a little surprised that only a single operator was working at what was clearly a busy airwave station, but she also knew that even if it wasn't busy, it could take some time before she received responses. Chickie held the level of status that meant any messages addressed to him would immediately be delivered to his house, but if he were out or asleep, he might not see the message for hours. Narci might have once held a similar status within the Air Fleet, but Svetlana suspected the situation had changed for her former lover.

The inhabitants of a nearby bench rose when the operator called out, "Message from Violetta Hampton," and Svetlana took the opportunity to sit. She waved to Deliah, who joined her on the bench a moment later.

"Anything from the ghosts?" Svetlana asked.

"Not yet. Could be days."

"Yeah, this might take days too. We'll wait half an hour or so," Svetlana suggested, glancing up at the clock above the airwave machine, "and then we can have the messages held. I'm ready to get back to where the air is fresh."

"Me too," Deliah said. "I can help Indy."

Svetlana nodded. "I'm sure he'll appreciate the help."

Before too much time had passed, the operator called out, "Message from Lord Algernon Boughorpington the Third?"

Svetlana leapt up from the bench and pushed her way through to the counter, holding out a hand for the message.

Chickie's response was brief. "No word since expedition announcement."

Svetlana folded the slip of paper neatly and tucked it into her pocket, just as the operator said, "And for a C. Marsh?", handing her another slip. Nodding at that, she took the second paper.

The message was not from Narci, but said, simply, "Returned. No longer with Air Fleet."

Svetlana's stomach dropped, as though the platform city had plunged toward the ocean without support of engines or a geyser. Narci had been a steadfast devotee of the Air Fleet for so long, and she had sworn she would not quit. If she was no longer there, it meant she had been forced out, likely because the Air Fleet no longer saw her as an asset, but a liability. Racking her brain to think if there was any other way to reach her friend, Svetlana came up with no other possibilities. She would have to wait until Narci found a way to contact her in order to get the full story. In the meantime, all she could do was worry.

CHAPTER FIVE

Athos squeezed Svetlana's shoulder when she told him the news about Narci. "She'll be alright, Sveta. Regardless of what happened, I have no doubt she's going to land on her feet."

"That's all fine and well," Svetlana said, "but I'd still like to know what's happening."

"The last delivery of parts is going to be here in half an hour. That's not nearly enough time for me to—" Athos trailed off, looking at Jo. "I won't be able to get any information without actually going to Heliopolis."

Jo shook her head, and Svetlana joined in. "At this point, we might not get back to Heliopolis again."

"That's a pity. I'll miss some of my friends," Athos said. "Speaking of, have you talked to Chickie?"

"He hasn't heard from her either. I can only guess she left in a hurry."

"You could send a message to Lar and see if he can send a ship over there."

Svetlana frowned. She didn't want her first words to Lar after their fight to be asking him for a favor, especially when she was still upset by his offer of a bride gift. He was probably still upset at her "idle rich" comment as well. Some time apart might do them some good, even though she did miss him.

Right now, her concern was greater for Narci, who had hung all her hopes on the Air Fleet and was now without the place she'd called home for her entire adult life. Athos was right about Narci, however. She was clever and resourceful, and there was not much sense to Svetlana worrying about her. Narci would figure out what she needed to do, and she'd get in touch with Svetlana when she was ready.

"I could. But I'm not going to. Let's just get back to Dougou so Indy can build his underwater contraption," Svetlana said.

Athos nodded and headed down the back stairs to help Deliah prepare the ship to leave. Jo tinkered with a few of the switches on the bridge while Svetlana stared out the windows. Her emotions were oscillating wildly between anger and longing for Lar, and worry and admiration for Narci. When she and Narci had split up a decade and a half ago, both had agreed it was a good thing for their careers and their lives, but that didn't keep Svetlana from wondering how different her life might have been if she'd stayed closer to Air Fleet Headquarters with Narci, or if Narci had been more inclined to life on a ship. Would they still be together, and far away from this current mess?

A scratching sound brought her attention back before she got too far into woolgathering, and she walked over to see what Jo had written.

"Leave a message in case she winds up here?"

Svetlana shook her head. "I don't know why she would, and I'm not sure I want to leave behind too many traces of us for anyone to pick up."

Jo nodded.

"Ready to fly, Captain," Athos called up through the speaking tube.

~

Annette greeted the crew as they returned to Dougou. "What's the good news, Captain?"

Svetlana glanced at Jo before returning her attention to the doctor. "We got the stuff Indy wanted?"

With a frown, Annette asked, "Did you get ahold of Narci?"

"No. She's not with the Air Fleet anymore," Svetlana said, "so we've got no news on whether they're getting ready to move platforms. We're flying blind."

"Ouch," Annette said. "Are you alright?"

Svetlana shrugged. "Just some devastating guilt over getting her into this situation, which I'm sure she'd tell me isn't my fault. Tell me you've got good news?"

"I do. If you got all the pieces Indy asked for, he and Drassilis should be ready to install them. I suppose we won't know for certain if this will work until we can test it, but the ideas have all been sound."

Svetlana gave Annette a thin smile. "Then that's better than nothing."

Athos and Deliah descended from the ship carrying a crate between them, both of them festooned with coils of rope and some sort of metallic tubing. "Give us a hand, ladies?" Athos asked.

Annette and Jo accepted some of the load from Deliah's arms and shoulders, while Svetlana did the same for Athos. Then Annette led them all through the village.

Deliah paused when they neared an animal pen surrounded by a wooden fence. She cocked her head to the side, looking at the tall, wooly animals within. "What are those?"

"Llamas," Annette said. "Don't get too close, Deliah. They aren't always friendly."

As if to emphasize her point, one of the llamas near the fenceline spat a mouthful of grain at one of its fellows, who skittered away. As the llama turned back to its meal, it showed the right side of its head with a puckered scar where its eye had once been.

Athos burst out in laughter. "Oh, Sveta, I'm sorry. I don't know if they name their animals here, but I'm calling that one Svetllama."

Svetlana leveled a glare at Athos, but the corners of her mouth tugged up nonetheless. "Hey, don't get between a one-eyed lady and her food."

"Point taken," Athos said, tugging his side of the crate that he and Deliah were carrying, pulling the girl farther from the fence. "Listen to the Captain, Deliah. She knows what she's talking about."

"I know," Deliah said, following Athos's lead. "She's my favorite captain."

Svetlana cocked her head to the side, her smile broadening. "Aw, Deliah, that's sweet of you to say."

"True, too. You don't stink or yell at me, much."

"Such standards," Annette murmured under her breath, her eyes twinkling with merriment. The conversation seemed to have put them all in good spirits, making their walk to the field where Indigo and Drassilis were working a little more pleasant.

~

After four days of Indigo, Drassilis, and assorted other members of the crew hard at work, the diving bell was starting to look like something that could withstand the pressures of the deep seas. Svetlana had done her part to help, but she'd proven unskilled at welding, which was the bulk of the remaining work at this point. She, Athos, and Jo had all been sent back to *The Silent Monsoon* early in the afternoon—Jo to rest and Athos to make sure that Jo followed Annette's orders—but now she found herself at loose ends.

She'd reviewed every scrap of paper, parchment, and even film from Lady de Whittvy's house, trying to ensure that they hadn't missed anything in their determination of the location of the Last Emperor's Hoard. Her mind kept wandering off the topic at hand, however. She'd replayed her argument with Lar in her head dozens of times, and the more she thought about it, the more she recognized that they'd never gotten to the point of discussing what was bothering her. Part of her wanted to fly back to Rrusadon to finish the conversation and reach a satisfactory conclusion, but the treasure needed to be her priority, no matter how much her heart longed to end her fight with Lar.

Athos's quiet entrance on the bridge might not have disturbed her on a normal day, but today, her subconscious mind focused on him and dragged her from her thoughts. His expression was solemn, and he looked as though he was trying not to bother Svetlana. When he noticed her looking straight at him, he asked, "You busy?"

"Not even remotely," Svetlana said. "What's on your mind?"

"This Gem of the Seas. Jo and I have been discussing it a little. When we find it, what are we going to do with it?"

Svetlana frowned. "I haven't really thought about that. I've been so focused on finding it before anyone else does that I haven't put much thought into what happens if we win."

"If the poem or prophecy or whatever that is written on the bottom of the map is correct, I don't think simply finding it is going to qualify as a win. We're going to have to keep it safe, or we'll have people coming after us to get it for the rest of our days."

"Yeah, I'd like to avoid being on the run forever," Svetlana said. "Wouldn't it be nice if we could somehow use it to keep ourselves alive and comfortable?"

Athos looked out toward Dougou and shrugged. "There's some appeal to that, yeah, but our luck says that won't happen."

"Agreed. Did you and Jo come up with any ideas?"

"Our best guess is that anyone else who wants to get their hands on the Gem is going to use it to drop the platform cities into the ocean. We can assume they'll either not bother evacuating anyone or they'll only evacuate a select group of people." Athos shook his head. "That's not what we want."

"Definitely not," Svetlana agreed. "We could use it to set things back to right, but only after we evacuated the platform cities."

Athos nodded. "That's one option, yes. But I don't think it's one that would make our lives easier in a hurry. We'd still be targets."

"Sounds like you've got another thought?"

"Jo and I came up with one idea, but we're not sure it's any better." He paused, taking a deep breath. "We could destroy it."

Svetlana stared at Athos, hardly believing what he'd just said. "Would that even ... what would that do?"

Athos shrugged. "That's what we don't know. We're putting a lot of faith into the idea that this Gem really is the reason why the oceans boiled. I can accept that it's true, but I could also believe it's a lie we've been fed. Maybe having it does nothing at all, and maybe destroying it does nothing either." He shrugged again. "Or maybe destroying it winds up worse than keeping it around. We don't know enough to be sure."

"Well, I'd certainly rather us be the ones who find out than leave it in anyone else's hands. There's a certain appeal to being rid of the thing and not allowing anyone else to use it either. But if that would put people in danger—" Svetlana shook her head. "—then I'm not interested."

"Then I think we're all on the same page, since I'd wager Doc would agree that keeping people safe is our main objective."

Svetlana nodded. "That she would. So we find it and we figure out what it really does. Hopefully."

"Agreed." Athos looked out the window again, sighing quietly. "We just have to hope that this delay isn't going to put us out of the running."

~

The diving bell was complete a few days later. Indigo looked as though he hadn't slept the night before, and Deliah scurried off to bring him a large mug of the strong tea they brewed in the village.

Jo poked at the door to the outer shell and then frowned. She wrote a note and held it up. "That door is going to keep the ocean out?"

Indigo nodded vigorously. "It has to. Or you die from the pressure."

Svetlana ran her hand across the rubber surrounding the door. "This is new?"

"Yes, Captain Tereshchenko," Drassilis said. "We replaced the seals on the door and windows. We also added metal plating around both to protect the rubber."

Svetlana nodded. "This is excellent, both of you." She turned to Annette. "Thank you, too."

Annette shrugged. "All I did was remind them that whoever goes down is going to have to breathe and not get wet. They pretty much figured out the rest themselves."

"So now we load this onto the ship and leap into the ocean?" Athos asked.

With a shake of her head, Annette said, "We'll run a few more tests while we're on the way. Nobody's jumping into anything yet."

"And I think we should get a little closer to the treasure, first," Svetlana said, smirking at Athos. "We can stop off at Anghor Tham to refuel and resupply before we head out into the great unknown."

~

Svetlana was manning the bridge alone, letting Jo have some needed rest, when Annette came onto the bridge. Her eyes were wide and her breathing heavy. A new development was about to ruin Svetlana's day, she suspected. "What is it?"

"We did our first tests on the diving bell, just sitting inside it for a few minutes with the doors closed." Annette forced her breathing to slow. "Indy rigged up an air circulator, but it doesn't make the air breathable. After a while, you start gasping like a dying fish. We need something that can actually recycle the air."

"How much work is that going to take?" Svetlana asked, wincing at the thought of additional delay.

"If we had the parts on board, Indy and Drassilis assured me they could have it done before we reach Anghor Tham."

Svetlana sighed. "I take it we don't have the parts?"

Annette shook her head. "No. It's some specialized equipment, and honestly, I don't think they can make it small enough to work with the diving bell. There is another option, though."

"Is that one any better news?"

"Not really. The alternative is to get tubing that can withstand ocean temperatures and pressure, and enough of it so we can keep the ship a safe distance away from the water. But we don't have that either. Or, rather, not without debilitating the *Monsoon*."

"Something like the tubing that takes the steam to the balloons and the condensation back to the steam tanks?" Svetlana asked.

"Yeah, that's exactly what Indy suggested."

"And where does he want us to find it?"

Annette winced. "You aren't going to like it."

"No, I probably won't," Svetlana said. Supplies like that weren't the sort of thing you could raid another ship for, unless you found an abandoned wreck with its hull still intact. And the only way to find an abandoned wreck like that was to be responsible for its demise.

"Athos suggested the Unfathomed Enclave."

"Yeah, Athos doesn't really know Dargon," Svetlana muttered, "but he's right. It's the best bet for parts in this chunk of the world. We can check at Anghor Tham first, since we're already headed there, but I suspect we're going to need to see Dargon after that."

~

Svetlana and Deliah stepped off the gangplank of *The Silent Monsoon* ahead of the rest of the crew. The moment Deliah's leading foot touched the platform, she made a gurgling noise and collapsed toward Svetlana.

Svetlana caught the girl beneath her arms and supported Deliah's head against her torso. Deliah's eyes were wide open but unfocused, her gaze darting erratically.

Annette pushed past Athos and Jo and rushed to Svetlana's side, looking over Deliah's prone body. "She's having some sort of a fit." She reached toward Deliah's feet.

"Wait," Svetlana said. "This might be the ghosts communicating with her. She said it works better on a platform. Can we give it just a moment?"

Annette frowned but nodded. "Lower her down to the ground, then, and turn her on her side. Just in case it's not her Aetherwave."

Svetlana did as she had been requested, crouching on the ground to keep Deliah's head off the dirt. She was keenly aware of the gazes of her crew and many passers-by. Thus far, Deliah had only made soft noises, and no coherent words had escaped her lips.

Annette sat beside Svetlana, legs crossed, keeping her gaze firmly on Deliah. She'd pulled out a pocketwatch but didn't consult it.

Before Svetlana asked the doctor about the watch, Deliah's entire body shuddered, and then the girl sat, rubbing at her eyes and looking around. "Oh. Anghor Tham."

"Yes, we've landed," Svetlana said, brow furrowing. The crew had spoken about the stop en route, and Deliah couldn't fail to have noticed that the ship had docked, since she'd walked down the gangplank. "Are you alright?"

Deliah nodded. "Little fuzzy. Ghosts won't meet."

"That was their message?" Svetlana asked.

Deliah nodded again.

"Did you find out where they are?" Athos asked, he and Jo now having joined the others at the bottom of the gangplank.

"Bonebriar."

"For the last cask," Annette murmured.

"No, an anchor point," Deliah replied.

Indigo shoved between Athos and Jo and scrambled across the dirt to Deliah's side. "Are you okay?"

Deliah nodded and pressed her hand into one of Indigo's.

"What's an anchor point?" Svetlana asked. "Anyone?"

"So the ghost ship doesn't drift," Deliah said.

"Drift where?" Annette asked.

"Off course," Indigo replied. "Right? Like old boats?"

Jo held up her notebook, which read, "Like mooring lines."

Deliah smiled. "I think so."

Svetlana frowned. The idea of an anchor point hadn't come up before, but if a ghost ship required a place to be attached to, Bonebriar wasn't too far from the reported location of the Last Emperor's Hoard.

"So we're going to have the Air Fleet at Barkovia and the ghosts at Bonebriar, and a whole lot of ocean in between for us to cover," Svetlana said. "I didn't really think we'd get out of this without going to the Unfathomed Enclave. I just hoped we could sort of skirt the edges, at best. Maybe wave politely."

"Unless they've started aerial trading, I don't think we're going to manage that," Athos said.

Jo handed Athos her notebook and started back up the gangplank.

"Ah, Jo says we should resupply on fresh water, and see if we can get some cargo here. 'Dargon likes plums'?" Athos frowned at the sentence he had read. "Alright, I'll see about some plums."

Svetlana shook her head. "Not plums. Plum wines."

Athos wrinkled his nose. "People drink those? Willingly?"

"Some people," Svetlana said. "Dargon, in particular. It looks like we're going to have to play nice with him, so we might as well bring him something to start us off on the right foot."

~

Simply flying toward the Unfathomed Enclave made Svetlana's stomach clench. What were once towering mountain peaks dotted the water, with only their uppermost reaches forming a collection of islands surrounded by the frothy waves of the boiling ocean. The ones closest to each other were connected by narrow bridges that looked as though a fierce windstorm might rip them away from their moorings. The ones spaced more distantly had a steady stream of small airships moving amidst them.

In the center of it all was Dargon's citadel. A flat plateau rose out of the ring of mountain peaks turned islands and played host to the largest and most elaborate buildings in the archipelago. A sane ruler would have put his citadel there, in the center of the largest city in the Unfathomed Enclave.

Instead, just to one side of the plateau, was the rest of what had once been the highest peak of the range. Sheared off and inverted, it was an upside-down mountain, hovering tenuously above a geyser. The former peak had been outfitted with engines and stabilizers to keep it hovering when the geyser was not active, but it had developed a slight cant to its bearing, leaving all the buildings atop it standing not entirely upright.

Jo brought the airship in close to the platform city, her jaw clenched tight. Tears glistened in the corners of her eyes, and her hands were bone white as they gripped the controls. She'd agreed to take a break from her pain medication regimen to steer the ship into port here, since Svetlana and Athos both felt ill-equipped to make this docking.

A creaking sound loud enough to be heard over *The Silent Monsoon*'s engines and through the windows of the bridge sent a shiver up Svetlana's spine. She balled her hands into tight fists. "You want help, Jo?"

Jo gave Svetlana a terse nod, and then jerked her chin toward the directional controls.

Svetlana adjusted her monocular, the small goggle-like device that covered her blind eye and gave her a limited amount of vision on that side. She shoved her long bangs back behind it, since the directional controls put her bad eye beside Jo. With the pilot still unable to speak, this was the worst possible setup for them to maintain, but Svetlana preferred Jo on the altitude controls when coming in for a docking on a platform that sometimes pitched or rose in unpredictable ways.

After a tense moment, Jo finally relaxed as *The Silent Monsoon* settled on the docking struts. She locked the altitude controls in place and gestured for Svetlana to do the same with the directional controls. Then she wrote a quick note. "Tell Dargon I said hi. I'm staying with the boat."

"Ship's yours, then. I'm taking Athos and Annette and leaving the kids behind."

Jo rolled her eyes. "I'm not babysitting," she muttered through her teeth, her jaw still restrained with gauze.

"No, just making sure none of Dargon's people think we're an easy target." Svetlana unbuckled her gun belt and set it on the control panel. "Dargon will have us all searched anyway, so there's no real point in you not having all our guns."

Jo managed a quick smile as she pulled one of Svetlana's pistols out of its holster and examined it.

Svetlana left the bridge and joined Athos where he was lowering the gangplank. "That the bag for the plum wine?" she asked, gesturing toward an old rucksack near the gangplank motor.

"Yeah, a couple of bottles. I figured we'd hold back the rest as bargaining material."

"Good idea."

Annette joined the two of them on deck just as the gangplank settled into position. "So this is the citadel, eh?"

"Welcome to the strangest place you'll ever set foot," Svetlana said.

"Let you do the talking, till we get to the trading part, and then let Athos do the talking," Annette said, repeating the information Svetlana had shared with them en route. "Why are you bringing me along?"

"In case we get shot," Athos said, looking to Svetlana for confirmation.

Svetlana chuckled, but nodded.

"You said no guns," Annette said.

"None for us," Svetlana confirmed. "Dargon's folks will have guns aplenty."

Annette forced a smile. "Right. Try not to get shot?"

"Always," Svetlana agreed.

~

Svetlana's legs ached from having to constantly adjust to the shifting surface beneath her as they made their way to the actual citadel building, and then from having to stand and wait until Dargon was ready to see them. Being on an airship was far more stable and even than the citadel's unusual platform was. She had been breathing slowly and carefully the entire time, trying to keep her temper in check.

A blast of fragrant smoke tickled at her nostrils as one of Dargon's staff, a dark-skinned, middle-aged woman, approached. Dressed far too well to be a servant, Guaa was one of Dargon's most loyal lieutenants, who had been working for him for as long as Svetlana had known Dargon or Guaa.

Before Svetlana could address her, Guaa said, "'E'll see ya now," in a thickly accented voice that faintly approximated Dargon's own accent.

Svetlana, Athos, and Annette followed Guaa into what they believed would be Dargon's office. Svetlana hadn't been here for years, and now his office looked more like a throne room, with richly woven tapestries above long plank tables and a variety of people seated at benches behind the tables. Most of the people were eating or drinking, but a few watched the crew's progress across the room.

At the far end of the room, where they were headed, hung a cloud of the same fragrant smoke that had heralded the arrival of Dargon's lieutenant. In the midst of it, sprawled across a gem-encrusted golden throne, was Dargon, his thick black hair draped across his eyes as he lounged, smoking a thick cigar.

He rolled his head to the side lazily, revealing his bronze-colored skin, trimmed black goatee, and deep brown eyes. "Svetlana, love, so good to see you," he murmured.

"How high is he?" Annette whispered to Svetlana and Athos.

"Shh," Svetlana replied before turning her attention to Dargon. "Likewise. I don't think you've met my associates. Doctor Annette Campbell, and Athos Tucker, my first mate. Annette, Athos, this is Dargon."

"Charmed. But not the point. I hear you're in need of some assistance," he said, blowing out a plume of smoke that obscured his face again.

"We thought we'd start with a gift," Svetlana said, gesturing toward Athos.

"Hmmm, he's yummy, but—" Dargon began.

"Not me, alas," Athos said, pulling the plum wine from his bag. "Just a couple of bottles. More where they came from." He took a half step in Dargon's direction, then paused. "May I approach?"

Dargon shifted in his seat, taking a keen interest in the bottles that Athos held. His nostrils flared as he asked, "Where from?"

"Ipeh," Svetlana said, naming one of the villages known only for their production of Dargon's coveted plum wine. "In exchange for some information."

"Regarding?" Dargon asked, his gaze not moving from the bottles.

Pausing a moment for effect, Svetlana said, "The location of the wreck of the Last Emperor's Fleet."

Dargon let out a throaty chuckle that turned to outright laughter. "And what makes you think we've got any information on that, love? We don't go fishing around in the waters here. They're unfathomed."

"You didn't pick up a chair like that in any of the usual locations," Svetlana said, nodding toward Dargon's throne. "In fact, I'd say that's a new addition to your collection. Makes me think you've found something."

Dargon shrugged. "Flotsam and jetsam wash up on our shores all the bloody time. Sometimes, it's a nice posh chair that just needs a bit of reupholstering."

"Mm-hmm," Svetlana said, crossing her arms over her chest. "That hardly looks to be flotsam or jetsam, and certainly not light enough to drift."

"Bring me the wine, friend," Dargon said, turning his attention back to Athos.

Athos bristled only long enough for Svetlana to notice the change in his demeanor, but then sauntered forward to present Dargon the bottles from a graceful bowed position.

"What else have you brought me, Svetlana, love?" Dargon asked as he took one of the bottles from Athos and studied the color in the faint light filtering through the smoke.

"Trade goods from Anghor Tham, in exchange for some parts."

"Parts, eh? I've heard tell you have a genius mechanic on board your little boat." Dargon stroked his beard, his gaze still fixed on the wine bottle. "Is Jo still with you too?"

"Yes, Jo is still with my crew. She's sticking with the *Monsoon* on account of the shifting." Svetlana held out her hand and wobbled it from side to side.

"Ah, her loss," Dargon said. "I would have loved to see her again." He paused, dark eyes scanning Svetlana's face. "You didn't confirm your genius mechanic?"

"You didn't ask me to confirm that, just that you'd heard a rumor to that effect," Svetlana fired back. "But yes, the rumors are true enough."

"Then I've got a deal for you, love," Dargon said. "I'll tell you what we know about the Last Emperor's Hoard if you'll bring me back, say, three-quarters of the treasure you find?"

Annette scoffed lightly. "No wonder he's got a throne," she murmured.

"And if we can't find our way to it with your information?" Svetlana asked warily.

"Then—" Dargon steepled his fingers and tapped them against his lips. "Ooh, I know. Then Jo and your genius mechanic come work for me for a year instead."

"How's that fair if your information doesn't help us?" Athos asked.

Dargon squinted at Athos. "So like Jo, with her incessant nay-saying." He turned his attention back to Svetlana. "You know my information will be worthwhile."

"It has been in the past," Svetlana said, measuring her words carefully, "and I'll consider your offer. But for the time being, Athos is my quartermaster. Who shall I send him to speak with about the trade goods?"

Dargon sighed dramatically. "Taking all the fun out of the negotiating with me, I see how it is." He jerked his chin forward, and Guaa moved to his side. "My lieutenant will make the trade negotiations too. Seems only right, both our seconds?"

"Thank you," Svetlana said. "I'll be in touch."

"I'm sure you will be," Dargon said. "Be sure to tell Jo and your mechanic what I'm offering. They might just jump at the opportunity."

"They might," Svetlana agreed, before she turned on her heel and strode out of Dargon's throne room.

CHAPTER SIX

Jo was waiting on deck when Svetlana and Annette returned to *The Silent Monsoon.*

"Problem?" Svetlana asked, eyeing the pilot.

Jo shook her head, then frowned. "Where's Athos?" she asked.

"Dealing with Guaa," Svetlana replied.

Jo tried to smirk, but stopped before the expression caused her pain. She picked up her notebook and wrote a longer response. "Sure he's thrilled to get that job."

"Why's that?" Annette asked. "She seemed nice enough."

"You caught her accent, didn't you?" Svetlana asked. "She tries to sound like Dargon, like someone who's pretending to have a good education, but she's hard to understand with all those clipped consonants."

Jo murmured. "Or he'll speak like her. That's a good laugh."

Thundering came from below deck just before Indigo arrived, panting. "Air Fleet," he gasped.

Svetlana spun around, scanning the skies. She spotted the ship immediately and gasped, her good eye widening in surprise. "That's not just Air Fleet, Indy. It's the flagship." The ship's flag fluttered into view, showing the Republican crest in the center, plain to the eye even at this distance. All the Air Fleet's ships flew a similar flag, but only the flagship flew it so large.

"Then it's—" Annette began.

"Bobby, most likely," Svetlana confirmed.

Jo grabbed Svetlana's arm and murmured, "Scramble?"

Svetlana shook her head. "We're already covered up as best as we can be. The larger problem isn't them spotting the ship, it's someone running into Athos, and he's got no warning." She rubbed her hand over her face, considering her options. She and Jo were too wanted to go anywhere near Dargon's citadel if the Air Fleet was there. Indigo was too identifiable. Annette was the member of the regular crew least likely to get pinched by the Air Fleet, but Svetlana couldn't imagine sending the doctor into this tense of a situation.

Finally, she looked at Indigo. "Can you ask Deliah to come up here, quickly?" Then she turned to Jo. "I'm going to need some scarves for her. The more shimmer the better."

Jo nodded and headed onto the bridge, while Indigo ran back down the stairs mid-deck.

"Why send Deliah?" Annette asked.

"Because she's the least wanted of all of us," Svetlana said. "I don't like it one bit, but I can't be sure Athos is going to get any warning if he's with Guaa, working on trade arrangements. If Deliah can get word to Athos and get out, she'll be fine. Failing that, she'll be able to sneak in and get us information on what the Fleet's here for. Either way, she's unlikely to get noticed right now."

Annette nodded, though she frowned as she did. "I could go with her, if you want. I suspect Bobby would be hesitant to arrest me. A lot of the Fleet still has strong feelings about war widows, even if they are known associates of criminals."

"Considered, but I don't want you to risk it," Svetlana said. "If Deliah gets spotted, she can probably manage to wriggle her way back to safety. The rest of us are too noticeable, even if we are disguised."

Deliah came on deck and cocked her head to the side, looking at Svetlana expectantly.

"Deliah, Jo's bringing up some things to dress you up differently. We need you to take a message to Athos, if you can find him. If you can't, we need you to see what's going on at Dargon's citadel."

"The big one?" Deliah asked, her gaze flickering from Svetlana's face to the approaching Air Fleet flagship.

"Yeah, the big one. Do you think you can blend in there?"

Deliah nodded. "Find out what the Air Fleet wants?"

Svetlana nodded. "Yeah. If you get into any trouble at all, run, okay? If they follow you back here, we'll deal with it. I want you to stay safe, no matter what."

"Aye, Captain," Deliah said.

Jo returned with an armful of scarves and a large brimmed, feathered hat sat jauntily atop her head.

"No hat," Svetlana said, grabbing it from Jo before Deliah could reach up for it.

Jo shrugged as she set to work covering up Deliah's bright colored pigtails and freckled young face with scarves in brilliant jewel tones. By the time she was done, Deliah looked like she had gained half again her body weight.

"Give me a moment," Annette said, hurrying below deck.

"Really warm," Deliah said, her voice muffled behind the scarves.

With a nod, Jo made some adjustments to the scarves, then looked at Deliah for approval.

"Okay," Deliah said, though her voice sounded a bit strained.

Annette returned with a small makeup bag. She adjusted the scarves over Deliah's face a bit and applied lipstick and eyeliner to the young girl's face, following it up with a quick dusting of a soft brown powder.

Deliah wrinkled her nose, but when she settled back into a more neutral expression, she looked quite different than she normally looked, far older than a teenaged street urchin.

"Try not to sneeze," Annette said. "It's not the right color for your complexion, but I don't think we've got—" She trailed off. "Nothing quite so light as your skin."

"Okay," Deliah said again. Her voice still sounded young, belying her appearance.

"Alright, go," Svetlana said. "Keep quiet if you can. We'll post Indy near the entrance to the docks to see you when you come back."

Deliah nodded and then hurried down the gangplank.

~

After close to an hour of pacing the deck, Svetlana spotted Indy, followed by Athos and Deliah's still-bundled form hurrying back to the ship. When Athos was halfway up the gangplank, she asked, "Was it him?"

She didn't have to specify who she meant. Athos nodded. "And a bunch of other high-ranking Fleet officers."

"How much did you overhear?"

"Not much." Athos gestured at Deliah. "She got in and found me fast, and I thought it prudent to get out of there as quickly as I could, before I got spotted."

"You're right, it's probably not safe for you to stay in there." Svetlana shook her head. "Probably not safe for me to go in there either."

Athos crossed his arms over his chest. "No, it's not. He's not here to welcome you back with open arms, Sveta. I know that much without hearing a word of the conversation."

"I need to know what they're discussing," Svetlana said, resuming her pacing.

"Send Deliah back in, then," Athos suggested. "She won't be noticed, especially in all that frippery."

"What makes you think I would be noticed, if I were similarly dressed?"

Athos rolled his eyes. "Oh, Sveta. Bobby would know. Or Dargon would figure it out and sell you out. He's not our friend."

"He could be, though," Svetlana said. "You were there. He offered us information in exchange for treasure. I'm sure the Gem of the Seas can stay in our twenty-five percent."

"Yeah, but if we don't get it, he gets Jo and Indy for a year."

"Then we'll stay too," Svetlana said.

Athos stared at her for a long minute. "You're done with Lar, then?"

Svetlana grimaced. She was still undecided on where her feelings for Lar stood at the moment. But with the Air Fleet here, reaching a conclusion on that front was low on her list of priorities. "I'll sort that out later, Athos. This is more important. I need to get word to Dargon, and I need to do it fast. Deliah, give me those scarves. I'm going in."

~

Svetlana crept through the halls of Dargon's citadel. The scarves and the affected hunch she walked with made her virtually unrecognizable, but it also made it impossible for her to see more than a foot or two in front of her at a time. All she needed to do was find Guaa or make it to Dargon's throne room to agree to Dargon's deal.

The rapid clack of boots on stone to her right gave her only a moment's warning before someone collided with her, knocking her off balance and throwing her attire into disarray.

"Pardon me, ma'am," a deep voice said, and a brown hand reached down to help her up.

Svetlana kept her head down, readjusting the borrowed scarves as she regained her feet, keeping both her eyepatch and her golden eye covered as she muttered her thanks to the person who had assisted her. She knew it wasn't Bobby, simply by the hand, but the cuff just above that hand was the navy blue of the Air Fleet, and she knew better than to make eye contact and give her identity away.

"Are you alright?" the voice asked.

"Just turned around," she murmured.

"Might I be of assistance, then? What are you looking for?"

"Guaa," Svetlana said.

The hand, still holding hers, tensed. "I'm sorry, who?"

Svetlana repeated the name, slightly louder this time.

The grip on her hand tightened and pulled her closer, as the other hand grasped at the scarves atop Svetlana's head.

Svetlana lashed out with her free hand, knocking away the hand attempting to remove her disguise. She ducked at the same time, trying to pull away from her assailant.

The other person kept a firm grasp on Svetlana, preventing her escape. Their opposite hand grabbed again at the scarves, this time with less delicacy than previously.

Svetlana wriggled to try to loosen their grip. She kept her face turned away from the aeronaut but couldn't keep her head itself out of the person's reach. The scarves fell away from her head and shoulders, and Svetlana found herself looking up at a face she dimly recognized. It was one of the female ensigns who had been in the Aetherwhere Division when she had left Narci behind.

"You're her," the tall, deep-voiced woman said, glaring at Svetlana with deep brown narrowed eyes. "Svetlana Tereshchenko." Without another word, the woman squeezed Svetlana's wrist and tugged her in the direction Svetlana had been headed, toward Dargon's throne room.

Svetlana got a glimpse of the woman's nameplate. "Captain Chaudhary, I'm afraid we got off on the wrong foot."

Captain Chaudhary scoffed. She was taller and stronger than Svetlana, so pulling the smaller woman along behind her barely slowed her stride, no matter how much Svetlana struggled. "Tell that to Admiral Beauregard."

"I really don't think that's a good idea." Svetlana struggled against Chaudhary's vice-like grip, which served to do nothing more than chafe the skin on her wrist.

"Oh, I'm certain he'll be thrilled to see you."

Unable to escape Chaudhary's grasp, Svetlana gave herself a moment to set her left foot, then drove her right foot into the back of the Air Fleet officer's knee.

Chaudhary stumbled. Her grip remained tight around Svetlana's wrist, and she turned back to look at her captive with a snarl, raising her opposite fist. "Give it up, Tereshchenko. I've dealt with far more dangerous criminals than you."

Without even a knife on her, Svetlana was at a disadvantage. Captain Chaudhary had a long reach, keeping Svetlana far enough away from her body that any attempts Svetlana made to hit her would be weak, at best.

Chaudhary had probably, however, been in fewer dirty fights than Svetlana had.

Svetlana crouched, again pulling against Chaudhary's hold on her. With her center of gravity lowered, she spun and pulled the other woman toward the corridor wall.

Chaudhary's shoulder impacted the wall and she released a loud "oof," but her grip on Svetlana's wrist did not waver. Her free arm swung for Svetlana's head and missed.

Svetlana's free hand shot upward and grabbed Captain Chaudhary's right wrist, the one that was preventing her escape. She dug her fingertips into the sliver of flesh between hand and jacket sleeve, her ragged nails adding little to the pain she might inflict in such a manner.

The Air Fleet Officer's second punch landed on Svetlana's temple.

Svetlana shook her head, trying to clear the blurriness that followed. She kept her grip on Chaudhary's wrist, but it loosened enough that her fingertips no longer indented the other woman's skin.

"Are we done?" Captain Chaudhary asked.

"I can keep this up all day," Svetlana said. The slight slur in her speech alarmed her, but she kept her cocky grin from slipping.

Chaudhary cuffed Svetlana again, this time on the jaw.

The pain radiated through Svetlana's head, and she released her grip on Chaudhary's wrist.

"Much better." Captain Chaudhary tugged Svetlana's arm and grabbed at Svetlana's other wrist. With her hands locked around both of Svetlana's slim wrists, Captain Chaudhary dragged Svetlana behind her.

Svetlana hardened her voice, with no semblance of a plea in her tone. "You could just let me walk away. It's not going to go well for you if you don't."

"We'll see about that."

~

All Dargon's people and the Air Fleet personnel assembled in his throne room looked up when Captain Chaudhary yanked open the door and pushed Svetlana forward.

The few remaining scarves around Svetlana's head fell mostly away with the motion, but Captain Chaudhary kept a grip on the one wrapped around Svetlana's neck. As it pulled tight against her windpipe, Svetlana coughed and clawed at it, trying not to look at anyone in particular as she did.

"I found her wandering the halls, Admiral," Captain Chaudhary said.

"She's—" Dargon began, but then stopped, squinting at Svetlana. "You know, I'm not sure where her loyalties lie, Admiral."

Svetlana widened her good eye and tried to speak, but she could only choke out a faint gasp for air.

Bobby finally looked at her. "Sveta." His gaze flickered behind her to Captain Chaudhary, but he didn't give his subordinate any commands about not strangling his former protégé. "You're going to have to come with me. I can't let you go like we did with Rear Admiral Marsh."

Svetlana tried to shake her head. She wanted to ask Bobby about Narci. Every time she tried to move, Captain Chaudhary seemed to tighten the scarf around Svetlana's neck. Breathing out through her nose, Svetlana stepped backward, trying to gain some slack. As the scarf loosened, Svetlana buckled her knees, ducking out of the makeshift noose and stumbling away from Captain Chaudhary, directly toward Bobby.

Three ensigns stepped between her and the Admiral, pistols drawn, all leveled at her head and chest.

Svetlana put her hands up. "What happened to Narci?" she asked. Part of her mind screamed at her that she should tell Dargon she was taking his offer before she checked up on Narci, but her heart wouldn't allow it.

"Aiding and abetting a known criminal is an offense that requires dismissal from the Air Fleet." Bobby's voice was measured. He barely made eye contact with Svetlana as he spoke. "Bind her," he said to one of the other Air Fleet officers.

"Wait, Dargon—" Svetlana shouted.

Before she could finish, something behind her exploded, and the Air Fleet personnel in front of her ducked or found the nearest cover. Svetlana crouched, twisting to the side as she did.

Smoke filled the air in Dargon's throne room, far thicker than what came from the end of his cigars. It carried with it an acrid odor, like burning rancid oil. Svetlana tucked her head down, breathing shallowly through one of her borrowed scarves, and waited for the smoke to clear.

Drassilis rolled through the doorway, dark gray smoke billowing from one of his hands, which he waved around. Svetlana couldn't tell if the automaton had caught fire, or if this was part of a diversion.

She had her answer a moment later, when Athos poked his head out from behind the automaton. "She's here!"

From somewhere within the smoke near Dargon's throne came a heavy coughing, followed by a gravelly voice saying, "Athos Tucker! Get him too!"

Svetlana turned back to Dargon. "Dargon! Is your offer still on the table?"

Dargon blinked a few times and opened his mouth slightly, his brow furrowed.

Something bumped Svetlana's foot, followed by an arm snaking around her waist. She struggled against the foreign grip.

"Captain Tereshchenko," Drassilis said. "Please do not struggle."

Svetlana relaxed, but asked, "What are you doing?"

"Effecting a daring rescue, with the assistance of Athos and Jo," Drassilis said.

Before Svetlana could speak again, Drassilis rolled backward at a speed far higher than Svetlana had ever seen him move, pulling her away from Dargon and the Air Fleet.

CHAPTER SEVEN

The Air Fleet personnel in Dargon's throne room regained their wits before Drassilis could remove Svetlana. Dargon had rules about guns in his citadel, but it seemed those rules didn't apply to the Air Fleet. Pistols flew out of jackets, and bullets followed soon after.

"No shooting!" Dargon shouted, even as he took cover behind his throne, pistols in both hands.

"Drassilis, tell me you've got weapons?" Svetlana asked.

"I do not." The automaton rotated his upper torso so Svetlana was now facing the doorway, where Athos and Jo both crouched, their pistols in hand. "Athos and Jo, however, brought extras."

Svetlana reached toward her crew members, even as bullets pinged against Drassilis's back. Jo handed her a gun, but Athos shook his head.

"Just get her out of here, Drassilis," Athos grumbled, leaning in to take a shot, and then moving out of the doorway.

"No, turn me back around, Drassilis," Svetlana said, readying her pistol.

"I'm sorry, Captain Tereshchenko. Retreating seems to be the best option." Putting on another burst of speed, Drassilis rolled out of the throne room.

Behind them, the door slammed, and footsteps followed Drassilis down the hall. All along their path, members of Dargon's staff got out of their way, either fearing for their safety at the hands of the automaton rolling at what seemed to Svetlana to be an unsafe speed, or because she was flanked by pistol-toting members of her crew. Regardless of the reasoning, none offered any attempts to stop them from fleeing Dargon's citadel.

As soon as Drassilis set Svetlana down, she whirled to face Athos. "I assume there's a good reason you pulled me out of there before I could make a deal with Dargon?"

"We heard you got captured," Athos said. "Are you alright?"

"I'm fine," Svetlana said, rearranging her scarves to cover her head and face. "And while yes, it's technically accurate that I was captured, I had things under control. If you'd have given me one more minute, I would have had Dargon willing to stop the Air Fleet on our behalf."

"That might not be necessary," Athos said, pulling Svetlana close as they started back toward the ship. "After you took off, I hit the streets with Drassilis, figuring we might have to extract you. I talked to some Air Fleet personnel, and it looks like they haven't a clue where to look for the Hoard."

Svetlana arched her eyebrow at Athos. "Do you believe them? I know they don't have all the information we have, but there are only so many places to look."

With a shrug, Athos said, "I'm not a mind reader, but it sounds like the whole reason they're here is to see what information Dargon has. Not knowing what they discussed before you got there, they may have already come to an arrangement."

"Unlikely," Svetlana said. "I'm honestly a little surprised Dargon's people even let Air Fleet land here."

"When they bring the flagship, it's a little hard to say no."

Svetlana nodded. The Air Fleet's flagship was enormous, striking fear into the hearts of all who saw it. She'd had a few temporary postings on it early in her career with the Air Fleet, and people were right to fear its capabilities. Its permanent staff kept it moving like the well-oiled machine it was.

And that staff was substantial. "Hang on, I've got a thought. Flagship means there's a lot of Air Fleet personnel here. If you've seen them out and about, then command's granted shore leave. They're planning to be here for a bit."

Athos nodded. "Yeah, it certainly looks like it."

"Then we've got an opportunity to spread rumors. Specifically, *false* rumors."

Athos grinned. "Oh, now you're talking, Sveta. What do you suggest?"

"Throw them off the scent of the Hoard. If they're setting up in Barkovia and asking about directions here, they've got to know it's somewhere in the Southern Sea. We won't be able to send them too far off course, but we might be able to redirect their attentions. Say a bit closer to Bonebriar?"

"There's open space amongst the islands there," Athos said, nodding. "Kind of similar to here, probably was a mountain range once. It's plausible, I'd say."

Jo muttered, "Will they buy it, coming from us?"

A smile crept to Svetlana's lips. "No, they won't, but that just means we take it one step further. The information needs to come from Dargon's people. We'll find a couple of them we can pay off and get them to start talking about it while there's Air Fleet within earshot. It'll look a lot more convincing that way and harder to trace back to us."

"I think it'll work, Jo," Athos said. "They came here for information, so you know they'll be thirsty for it."

Jo shrugged, but ultimately nodded.

Athos grinned. "Drassilis, could you please get the Captain and Jo back to the ship safely? I've got some work to do."

~

Svetlana and Athos sat in the corner of The Raven and Lion, a bar that had attracted a large crowd of Air Fleet personnel enjoying their shore leave. Athos had spent the day getting the rumor mill moving, and now they waited to see the results of his work. That they could also enjoy mugs of the fruity-tasting beer that was popular in the Unfathomed Enclave while they waited was an added bonus.

The bar was far cleaner than Svetlana had expected, nothing like the seedy bars on Heliopolis where the crew of *The Silent Monsoon* often went for information or entertainment. The structure of the building itself was more like a tent, with sailcloth stitched together and stretched between metal and wooden poles, but the walls were clean and free from holes. The breeze flowed through the walls near the stitching. It was a warm evening, and the moving air kept the interior of the bar from smelling like the variety of alcohol served there.

It was also crowded enough that they could enjoy their drinks and observation unnoticed. Simply wearing hats that cast their faces in deep shadows was enough of a disguise for both Svetlana and Athos to be unnoticed by the Air Fleet personnel.

One of the serving girls approached them. Svetlana started to wave her away from their table, but the young woman, blonde, tanned, and lithe, smiled at Athos and moved around the table to crouch at his side.

"They're talking," the young woman murmured, loud enough that Svetlana could hear her.

Svetlana glanced at the young woman. "Oh, she's one of yours?" she asked Athos.

"Violet doesn't belong to anyone," Athos said, gesturing at the young woman. "She's agreed to bring me information, in exchange for us giving a generous donation to one of the local schools." As if to further emphasize his statement, Athos dropped a few coins into a high pocket on Violet's apron, centered just below the neckline of a dress that emphasized her chest.

"I see," Svetlana said, turning her attention fully to Violet, apparently named for the color of her eyes. "What are they talking about?"

"Bonebriar, of course," Violet replied. "It seems they may have left there too hastily to learn some of the mad scientist's secrets."

"Mad scientist?" Svetlana asked, arching an eyebrow at Athos.

Athos shrugged. "It's a slight embellishment, but I tried to put more emphasis on the 'scientist' part over the 'mad' part."

"Have any of them mentioned whether their shore leave is going to be cut short?" Svetlana asked.

Violet nodded. "They're none too happy about it, but it seems like the Fleet's sent out some morale boosters with the younger crew. Buying them lots of extra beer and leading them in rousing cheers about the good of the Republic." She cast a glance over her shoulder. "Speaking of, I'd best be getting back to bring them another round."

Athos nodded as Violet left, and then turned his attention to Svetlana. "It sounds like it's working."

"If they are actually leaving for Bonebriar soon, then word has made its way back to Bobby already."

Athos nodded again, scanning the crowd. "I would like to hear official word from someone in the Fleet. See anyone who won't arrest me on sight?"

Svetlana shook her head. "There's no one we can ask about their orders without getting pinched. Again, in my case."

"Fair," Athos said, stroking his goatee. "Then we take Violet's word for it?"

Svetlana nodded. "We can take the long way back to the ship and see if we hear confirmation while we're walking. And if not, we can hope someone else on the ship has turned something up."

~

Annette was the only member of the crew on the bridge of *The Silent Monsoon* when Svetlana and Athos returned. She had doused most of the lights on the ship, save for one lamp above her chair, which illuminated the book she was reading. She looked up as the captain and first mate entered the bridge. "Anything good?"

Svetlana shrugged. "The rumors are making their rounds. We don't have direct confirmation that the Air Fleet is leaving, but I suspect their ships will be gone by morning."

"Where's everyone else?" Athos asked.

"Indy and Deliah wanted to go to the market to look for parts, so I sent Jo with them," Annette replied. "She can still make them understand 'no' even if she isn't speaking much."

Athos chuckled. "Yes, she absolutely can." He turned to Svetlana. "So, what's next on the agenda?"

"We've got a general idea of where we need to go, but we need to pinpoint it more," Svetlana said. "Otherwise, it's like searching all of Bonebriar for a small coin. Maybe even harder."

"If Dargon doesn't have that information, who would?" Annette asked.

"We'd need older maps, I think," Svetlana said. "Ancient ones, really. I've seen some maps from when ships still sailed that talked about hazards and depths and such. No one cares about that anymore, but now we need to."

"Then what?" Athos asked. "Just pick out the likely locations based on centuries-old maps?"

"It would at least narrow it down," Svetlana said.

"Aside from a handful of maps that were reprinted in histories, the only place I know of that maintains those is the Air Fleet Academy," Annette said.

"Then let's see what we can find in your books first," Svetlana suggested. "If that doesn't hold water, we'll need to figure out what the Air Fleet really knows, outside of the bad rumors we've fed them."

Feet pounded up the gangplank, followed by a glimpse of blue and orange-yellow hair, and a moment later, Indigo and Deliah thundered on to the bridge. Glancing past them, Svetlana saw Jo bringing up the rear, carrying a bulging knapsack over her shoulder.

"Did you find what you need?" Svetlana asked Indigo.

"And more stuff too," Indigo replied, breathless.

"Like what?" Svetlana asked, her good eye narrowing.

Indigo gestured to Deliah, who was red faced and panting. The girl gulped at the air for a moment, then bent at the waist, putting her hands on her knees, and took several deep breaths. Finally, she straightened, her face now its normal pale, freckled shade.

Before she could speak, though, her body stiffened, her skin grew paler, and she began to fall. Indigo grabbed at her arm, but Athos stepped forward and caught her before she hit the floor.

"Ghosts," Indigo muttered, backing away from Deliah as he spoke.

Annette set down her book and crouched by Deliah's side, watching the girl's eyes shift back and forth. Deliah's eyelids remained open, and her eyes moved at an alarming rate.

Svetlana watched, her own limbs stiff as if reacting in sympathy to Deliah's rigid body. Deliah was certainly receiving some sort of communication from the ghosts, as Indigo had said, but this time seemed more violent than previously.

Her paralysis did not last long, and she slumped into Athos's arms almost as quickly as the seizure had begun.

Annette grabbed Deliah's wrist and felt for the girl's pulse, then put her head near Deliah's chest for a moment. "She's fine, but it knocked her out. That's new, right?"

Svetlana nodded. "Is it safe to move her?"

"It might be better if we can just make a little bed for her here. I don't know if she'll wake up rictus or thrashing. Or neither."

Annette shrugged. "This isn't something I've encountered before, so it's all guesswork from me."

"I'll get her pillow and blanket," Indigo said, already running toward the back stairs.

"She saw something on a map," Jo said, her voice muffled on account of her restrained jaw.

Svetlana looked at Jo. "An old map?"

Jo nodded. "I didn't see it. She'll have to explain it to you."

"Then let's hope she wakes up soon," Svetlana said.

CHAPTER EIGHT

Deliah thrashed awake, her limbs flailing in the blanket Indigo had covered her with. "They know," she gasped.

"Who knows?" Athos asked.

"The ghosts," Deliah and Svetlana said in unison.

"What did they find out, Deliah?" Svetlana bit the inside of her cheek as she awaited Deliah's response.

Panting briefly, Deliah licked her lips. "What I saw. Thirsty."

Annette handed Deliah a mug of water she'd brought up from the mess, and Deliah gulped it down.

"There's sea caves, and now the ghosts know too," the girl said after finishing the water.

"Sea caves?" Athos frowned. "What does that mean?"

"Like an underwater cave?" Annette asked.

Svetlana nodded. "Jo said you saw an old map. Did that have the sea caves?"

"On the map." Deliah nodded. "More water?"

Indigo took the mug from Deliah and hurried away.

"Okay, can you show us where these sea caves are, on the map here?" Svetlana asked.

Deliah rose and approached the map in the center of the bridge. She ran her fingertips across the surface near the Unfathomed Enclave, far on the left side of the map, then splayed one hand to bridge the gap between Dargon's territory and the island where Barkovia sat. Her other hand tapped on Bonebriar, near the right side of the map, before she slid both hands to the edges of the map. "Where the edges would meet."

Annette moved to a table covered in books and ran her finger along the spines. She pulled one from the stack, flipped it open, and rifled through the pages. When she reached the one she was looking for, she laid it on the table, pointing to the map there, which showed the world from a different perspective, placing Bonebriar, Barkovia, and the former mountain range that was now the Unfathomed Enclave in a rough triangle in the Southern Sea, their proximity clearer on this version of the map. "Does this help?" she asked.

Deliah nodded and pointed to a spot between the three. "Right about here. A little closer to the Un ... the mountain place."

Annette looked at Svetlana, arching her eyebrows. "That looks about right, doesn't it?"

Svetlana nodded, then turned her attention back to Deliah. "Did the map explain anything about what the sea caves are?"

Jo handed Svetlana a piece of paper with a couple of sketches and a handful of words. "Weird navigational symbols like these. Recognized a few. Choppy water, unexpected surges. Sounds like what happens near geysers."

Svetlana frowned as she read the note aloud, and then to herself several more times. She'd only studied sea navigation in the vaguest of ways, primarily in terms of how sea-based ships lent themselves well to aerodynamic airships, with their narrow prows, designed to cut through waves. Though the types of navigational hazards encountered on the ocean before the Boiling didn't make sense to her, they were not too unlike conditions she'd experienced while flying. She looked at Jo. "That's what some wind patterns do to us. Strong winds, in particular."

Jo nodded, then ran her fingertips over the map on the bridge. She tapped her fingers on several locations, each one bearing the words "strong winds."

"Does that mean there's a strong current there, too?" Athos asked.

"I can't say for certain," Svetlana said, "but it makes me think there are some sort of gusts there. Like gusts from beneath the water."

"Like bubbles in a tea pan," Indigo said as he returned with a mug of water for Deliah.

"Bubbles in a tea pan are from heated air moving to the top," Annette said, frowning at Indigo. "Not the water itself."

Svetlana's good eye widened. "But what if that's it? What if there are pockets of air trapped beneath the water, in these sea caves, that sometimes bubble up to the surface to create the navigational hazards?"

Athos shrugged. "What good would that do us? If the ocean's boiling like a tea pan, then the air's going to be hot, maybe too hot to breathe comfortably."

"But you *can* breathe hot air," Svetlana said. "Look, Indy's diving bell is going to get us down there, but the best we've got to collect the treasure is an imprecise net system. If we can leave the diving bell and breathe in these sea caves, we might have a better chance of reaching the Hoard."

"That sounds like more danger than I'm interested in," Athos said. "Back me up here, Doc?"

Annette frowned, her gaze somewhere in the distance. "I don't know for certain if the air would be breathable or not. What happens if the air pocket shifts and bubbles up to the surface? You'd be stranded at the bottom of the ocean, with no air to breathe, if the bubble isn't strong enough to buoy you up as well."

"Okay, my enthusiasm might be a little pre-emptive," Svetlana admitted, "but we're not going to find out anything until we get there." She looked at Deliah. "We're going to need a copy of the map so we can get coordinates. You and Jo head back over to where you saw it and make a copy, alright?"

Deliah nodded, and she and Jo left the bridge together.

"What about me, Captain?" Indigo asked, though his gaze was following Deliah toward the gangplank.

"I need your brain here," Svetlana said. "And unfortunately, I need your brain here when Deliah's isn't."

Indigo turned his attention back to Svetlana, one eyebrow arched, in a faint imitation of one of Athos's common expressions.

"You've seen how the ghosts can take over Deliah's brain now?" Svetlana asked. Without waiting for Indigo's response, she continued. "We need to find a way to prevent that."

Drassilis made a sound that resembled a human clearing their throat. "Captain Tereshchenko, I believe I may have a solution to offer. What you are asking to do is to block the transmission of what you call the Aetherwaves into Deliah's mind, yes?"

Svetlana nodded. "Something like that, yeah. Why, do you have an idea?"

"Mother and I were working on a method to prevent Aetherwhere from interacting with reality." He paused. "That is, of course, prior to her demise. I may be able to apply what we learned to this problem."

"Really?" Svetlana asked. "Odd line of study, but it sounds promising. Is that something you could build out of parts we've already got here?"

"Yes, I believe so," Drassilis replied. "Indigo and I have been organizing the parts in the engine room."

"Thank the Skyfather for that," Athos muttered. "I do have a question, though. If there's a way to block Aetherwhere, there'd be ways to get around that too, wouldn't there?"

"Perhaps," Drassilis admitted, "though Mother and I did not get that far with the devices we were developing."

Athos looked at Svetlana and shrugged. "I'm just thinking that if I came up with something that blocked Aetherwhere, and then I became part of Aetherwhere—like, say, a ghost—I'd want a way to unblock myself."

"It could be different on that side," Annette said. "It might be more useful for them to build something to keep reality out."

"If the ghosts are what's causing Deliah's fits, I think we should focus on doing something that might prevent them from contacting her," Svetlana said, her voice even. "It doesn't seem to be doing her any favors when they do, and I'd rather them not find out what we're doing. As it is, they could already be on their way to the sea caves, and they may be able to go underwater without any of our equipment."

Annette nodded. "Protecting Deliah from more of these seizures is valuable. At the very least, we should try."

Svetlana nodded, then turned back to Athos. "Anything else you want to add?"

Athos frowned. "Did you send Jo with Deliah so she couldn't get involved with this debate?"

"No, I sent her because she'll be able to find and retain the coordinates the best out of all of us," Svetlana said.

Athos grinned. "Okay, that makes better sense."

Svetlana smiled back. "Gotta keep on my toes with you lot. Alright, Indy, Drassilis, get started on something for Deliah to keep the ghosts out of her brain. Maybe make some extras, too, just in case. I might have an idea."

~

The Unfathomed Enclave was the sort of place where you could find anything you needed or wanted. Svetlana had proved the point by acquiring three old buoys, each about four times the size of her head, likely scavenged from the seas after the Boiling. They were flecked with rust and chipped paint, but she didn't need them to look pretty, just to float, and the merchant who sold them to her had proved they would.

She struggled down the stairs into the hold with them, banging the hollow metal balls off the walls several times before Athos and Jo poked their heads out of Athos's room.

"You need some help, Sveta?" Athos asked, his brow furrowed.

"Sure," Svetlana replied. "Each of you want to grab one of these and take them to the engine room?"

"What are they for?" Athos asked as he accepted one of the buoys from Svetlana.

"A net trap, metaphorically speaking."

Jo frowned deeply, but then her eyebrows shot up, eyes wide, and she nodded, tapping Athos's shoulder as she did.

"You're going to have to enlighten me on what a net trap is."

"Ancient fishing technique," Svetlana said, passing a buoy into Jo's waiting arms. "You put up some poles in the shape of a triangle and tie a net to all three. The net is underwater. So the fish swim in, but then they lose their way and can't get back out. You come back later and pull up the net full of fish."

Athos looked from Svetlana to Jo and then back to Svetlana. "But we don't want boiled fish."

"This isn't a net trap for fish. Step two is putting the anti-Aether devices that Indy and Drassilis are building onto each of the buoys and drop them near the sea caves. Assuming they work like I think they will, it will either keep the ghosts from getting too close, or trap them in the middle of it with no clear way out."

"Okay, assuming what they make works at all, I guess that could be useful. I just ... how do you even test something that prevents something you can't see?" Athos asked.

"Faith, I guess," Svetlana said. "Faith in science beating out the inexplicable weirdness of the world."

"Oh, good," Athos said, smirking. "Invoking the Skyfather on matters of the sea is always helpful."

Svetlana shrugged. "I know it's not his domain, but it wouldn't hurt if you want to spend some time praying. Personally, though, I'm counting on science, not the Skyfather, for this one."

~

With the addition of the anti-Aether device on *The Silent Monsoon*, the bridge was considerably more crowded than usual. Having Drassilis to monitor the device meant an extra body on the bridge, but the prototype anti-Aether device itself was also not small.

"We're going to be able to build those smaller to go on the buoys, right?" Athos asked, peering at the strange jumble of copper and wires that Indigo and Drassilis had insisted would keep the ghosts out of Deliah's brain.

"Indigo and Deliah are working on that presently," Drassilis said, his too-human eyes fixed on the small panel of gauges attached to the anti-Aether device. "Captain Tereshchenko, we appear to be at maximum operational capacity."

Svetlana glanced at Jo and shrugged. "I think that means go."

Jo nodded and released the last catch preventing the ship from moving, and they slipped away from the Unfathomed Enclave.

Drassilis rolled from the anti-Aether device to the cloud generator and made a humming sound that he occasionally made when he was thinking. The crew guessed he did it to make himself seem more human, but the oddity of the sound made it clearer that he was an automaton. "We will need to allow this device to grow warm before we can deploy it."

"Grow warm?" Svetlana asked. "You mean 'warm up'?"

"Quite right, Captain Tereshchenko," Drassilis said.

"That's fine, Drassilis. We won't need it up and running until we're out in the middle of the ocean, just a strange little raincloud dropping buoys into a random stretch of ocean."

Jo snorted out a chuckle.

"Feeling better, then?" Svetlana asked her.

Jo shrugged, but then nodded hesitantly. "Buoys dropping from a raincloud won't look suspicious at all."

"If we're lucky, no one will be there to see it," Svetlana countered.

"We're never that lucky," Jo said.

"Too bad the Kavisolis didn't install a waterspout disguise feature on this device," Svetlana said.

"We don't know that they didn't," Athos said, pointing at the button Indigo had fixated on earlier. "We still don't know what that does."

"Can we not press it just yet?" Svetlana asked. "I don't want to find out that it shuts the whole thing down for good when we might still have use for it."

Athos nodded. "I suppose that's only fair. Holler when we get near the drop point. I'm going to see how much size we can shave off the other anti-ghost things."

~

Even from within the wisps of an artificial cloud, Svetlana could see enough of the boiling water beneath her ship to be nervous about her plan. The buoys were designed to float, even with some additional weight on them, and they were meant to have a top and bottom that stayed in those positions. The anti-Aether devices that Indigo, Deliah, and Athos had constructed were smaller than the one on the bridge, and they had installed them so they should remain on the top portion of the buoys. But they were electronic devices. If the buoys rolled, the devices would be submerged, and none of the crew expected these small collections of spare parts to keep working if they were underwater.

Indigo joined Svetlana at the prow of the ship and looked down at the water. "Too high."

"We can't get much closer, Indy," Svetlana said. "The steam is bad enough here, and if we damage the hull, we'll have to go into landdock. We don't have time for that right now."

Nodding, Indigo walked over to one of the buoys and placed his hands on either side, rocking the sphere slightly. "Guess this has to work."

"I hope so," Svetlana said. She was sweating from the heat of the ocean, but also from her concerns over this plan. She wanted more time to make sure everything would work right, but with the ghosts closing in on this location, and the Air Fleet potentially close behind, they didn't have the time to spare. "Let's do this."

Together, Svetlana and Indigo lifted one of the buoys to a pincher claw at the end of a winch system they had set up on the deck, previously used for moving cargo on and off *The Silent Monsoon*. Once the buoy was suspended, Indigo moved to the controls and swung it out over the side of the ship, then lowered it as far as the rope and device would allow.

"Ready?" he asked, his high-pitched voice reedy and strained.

"Drop it," Svetlana said, watching the buoy over the side of the ship.

Indigo pressed the button to release the pincher claw, and the buoy dropped into the ocean. It bobbed up and down, tilting perilously as it did, but it came to rest with the anti-Aether device perched on top, a small green light blinking cheerily to indicate it was working.

"One down," Svetlana said, signaling to Jo on the bridge to move the ship. "Two to go."

CHAPTER NINE

Svetlana looked over the bulkhead at the three buoys, floating in a triangle near the coordinates where Deliah had identified the sea caves. They looked miniscule at this distance, even with *The Silent Monsoon* hovering near enough to the boiling sea to counteract the crisp autumn air with the water's heat and humidity. Their blinking was out of sync with one another, creating a slightly dizzying effect, but Indigo and Drassilis had assured Svetlana this wouldn't affect the way they worked.

Athos poked his head up from below. "Captain? Indy says we're ready to deploy the diving bell, but we need to do it from down here, and ... you're going to want to see this thing."

Svetlana arched her eyebrow. "I thought everything was fine."

"I have concerns." Athos ducked back down the staircase.

Svetlana followed him into the hold, where the diving bell took up the bulk of the space, stinking of welding, rubber, and some unidentifiable scents likely related to other work they'd put into the craft. She had seen the individual pieces before, but seeing it all put together was a different experience.

The diving bell was on its side, as it was too tall to stand upright in the hold. Upright, it would be twice as tall as she was, with tubes and ropes attached to pulleys extending off the top of it. The exterior was brushed dark silvery metal, with thick black rubber tubes surrounding windows made of glass so thick they obscured what was inside rather than providing a clear view.

Then again, there wasn't much to see inside. Svetlana knew a layer of coiled tubing ran beneath the surface of the outer diving bell, surrounding a smaller inner diving bell. From the outside, none of this was apparent, but Annette, Indigo, and Drassilis had explained it to her.

Seeing it in person made it suddenly more real, and she felt a hollow gnawing in her stomach. "I understand," she murmured to Athos. Turning to Indigo and forcing a smile, she asked, "Are you sure this is going to work?"

"Mostly sure," he said.

"The theory is sound," Annette said, "and as best as I can tell, the execution looks sound too. But I've proposed a test drop. Unmanned."

Despite her concerns about locating the Last Emperor's Hoard before the Air Fleet or the ghosts, Svetlana nodded quickly. "Yes, absolutely. We've got time for that. Even if we don't, we'll make time for that."

Indigo nodded. "Have to push it in."

Svetlana and Athos shared a sidelong glance, but stepped into place to help their lanky mechanic push the diving bell toward the opening in the wall of the hold, which was normally used for loading and unloading of larger cargo items, and normally when the ship was stationary at a dock, not hovering above the ocean. Indigo had set the diving bell on long wooden skids, so it wasn't as hard to push as Svetlana had originally expected, but it was still a heavy hunk of metal and tubing.

As they reached the edge of the hold, Svetlana cast a quick prayer skyward, though she knew they'd moved far from the Skyfather's realm of influence.

The diving bell swung out of the hold, still suspended by ropes above the open ocean below. Indigo ran to where the ropes were tied off and undid two of them, then held one out toward Athos.

Athos joined Indigo, and the two of them began to lower the diving bell into the boiling water, while Svetlana, Jo, Annette, and Deliah clustered around the open section of the hull to watch it go down.

The base of the diving bell impacted the water and bobbed, much like the buoys had, then began to sink beneath the waves almost immediately.

"It might just work," Annette murmured, a note of glee in her voice.

As the diving bell slid lower into the water, the waves reached one of the tubes atop the craft, designed to allow clean air to reach the inhabitants. What looked like a wisp of smoke or steam rose from the tube.

"What's that?" Svetlana asked, pointing it out to the rest of the women clustered at the door.

"Not good," Jo murmured.

"No, not good at all," Annette said, squinting downward. "Indy, hold there."

Indigo grunted assent, strain apparent even in his unvocalized word.

Svetlana turned to go help him, but Athos reached out his spare hand and helped Indigo hold the rope in place. "What's happening?"

"What's the tubing made of?" Svetlana asked Indigo.

"Copper coil," Indigo replied.

"Maybe not," Annette said, shaking her head. "Whatever it is, it's melting. Pull her back up."

Svetlana moved to help Indigo, while Jo joined Athos on his rope. The four of them made quick work of pulling the diving bell back up, but Svetlana's thoughts remained on the melting tubing. Had they not tested it, she and Athos could have been boiled alive by the ocean water leaking into the diving bell as they descended.

The craft reeked of the sulfurous scent of the ocean, but also of singed hair or flesh. And the air tube bore a small hole, wet around the edges, where it had melted.

"Tubes won't hold," Annette said.

"So we're back to the beginning?" Athos asked.

Annette shrugged. "We need something more durable."

Indigo joined her beside the diving bell and poked a broom handle at the edge of the hole. "Not copper."

"We need what we wanted in the first place," Svetlana said. "Where did we get that from?"

"Warehouse at the Unfathomed Enclave," Indigo replied.

Svetlana frowned. "Was it one of Dargon's warehouses?"

With a shrug, Indigo said, "I don't know. Small one."

"That doesn't sound like one of Dargon's, then," Svetlana said. "We may need to talk to him about more supplies."

Jo muttered, "Send Drass?"

Svetlana looked at Drassilis. "Do you think you could go in the diving bell? You don't ... do you breathe?"

"Yes, Captain Tereshchenko, I do breathe," Drassilis said. "I am also uncertain whether my construction could handle both the temperature and the pressure, even if there were a way to allow me to breathe. Unfortunately, the secondary diving bell entrance is smaller than my body."

"Then I suppose that's a 'no' to sending Drassilis." Svetlana shook her head. "We can't be sure we're getting the right stuff, unless we can get it from someone with a vested interest in us staying alive." Then she smirked. "I've got just the patron in mind."

~

The hallways of Dargon's citadel were now devoid of any Air Fleet presence, which allowed Svetlana to breathe easier as she strode down the hallway with Jo at her side. All around them, Dargon's people were whispering. *Let them*, she thought. *Let the rumors of our return reach his ears before we do.*

Guaa met them just outside of Dargon's throne room, shaking her head. "Both of you?"

"Jo hasn't seen Dargon in so long, she just couldn't be nearby and not pop in to say hello," Svetlana said.

Jo smiled broadly and waved.

Guaa looked at Jo and the bandages surrounding her head, then back at Svetlana. "Cat got her tongue?"

"Aldfort guards broke her jaw."

Guaa made a show of grimacing. "So that's true too then, eh? Got caught in the High Council's chambers with illicit information?"

Jo shook her head, but Svetlana responded. "Yes and no. It's hardly illicit information if it's on public display. It's just information they don't want publicly known at the moment. Especially not by our type." She gestured at the door. "Is your boss in? I've got business I need to discuss with him."

Crossing her arms over her chest, Guaa said, "He is, but he's not holding an audience right now. I can pass on a message to him."

"Not holding an audience? When does Dargon ever turn down an opportunity to be seen? Or are you trying to say he doesn't want to see us?"

"He doesn't want another incident like your most recent visit."

"Well, if he's not dealing with the Air Fleet currently, I can promise I'll be on my best behavior," Svetlana said, smiling.

"What about the rest of your crew?"

"Jo will behave too, and I don't have any automatons with smoke bombs waiting in the wings to rescue me." Svetlana gestured down the hallway in the direction they'd come from. "See, no automatons."

Guaa shook her head, eyes skyward as she did, but opened the door for Svetlana and Jo.

The throne room was far quieter than it had been on her two previous visits, most of Dargon's hangers-on having moved on to more productive uses of their time. Only Dargon and a couple of servants holding trays of food and drink remained in the room.

Dargon caught Svetlana's good eye and scrambled from his relaxed lounge across his throne to a seated position, though his muscles were tensed as though he would spring from his chair at any moment. "Guaa?" he called out.

"She promised not to bring a robot this time," Guaa called back, pulling the door shut.

Svetlana chuckled. "Not a fan of automatons?"

"Not a fan of yours," Dargon spat back. "That thing is ... what is that thing?" Then he paused, finally spotting Jo. "Oh, Josephine, so good to see you!"

Jo smiled and mocked a quick curtsey in Dargon's direction.

Dargon chuckled. "How utterly charming. You're here and you can't speak." He glanced at Svetlana. "Can I keep her?"

"She's not interested in being kept," Svetlana said, "but we're willing to negotiate your offer."

Dargon waved the servants away as he studied Svetlana and Jo. As they departed, his voice took on a cooler tone. "What are you two playing at?"

"We're not playing at anything," Svetlana said. "I came back earlier to accept your offer. The Air Fleet made that difficult, so Athos made the call to get me out of danger. Sorry about the mess. At this point, we're stuck. We need a little more, so we're offering a lot more."

Dargon's eyebrow arched. "Oh, do go on, Captain."

Svetlana paused before answering. She'd discussed the offer with her crew, but she still hated making it. If they hadn't been in a rush, she wouldn't have suggested it at all. She would have gone back to Rrusadon, hashed out the "bride gift" nonsense with Lar, and gotten Kavisoli assistance with the next part of the plan. But she couldn't spare the time, not when Dargon was right here and was certain to have what they needed, so close to where they needed to travel next. Plus, he was greedy enough to jump on this deal. "We're still offering 75 percent of whatever we find, but if we come up empty, then you'll have the services of my entire crew and my ship for a year and a day."

Dargon might have had the ability to conceal his motivations if he were playing cards or conducting negotiations, but when someone was presenting him more than what he wanted, he clearly saw no need to pretend. "Delightful. And what do you want from me?"

"In exchange for the added value, we need access to your warehouses for parts to make the dive."

"You're awfully certain of this treasure, aren't you, Captain?" Dargon asked.

"Certain enough to make the offer," Svetlana said, her voice strained.

Dargon's gaze flickered over Jo, clearly trying to read her body language. For her part, Jo stood fairly relaxed, almost casual, but tense enough to meet Dargon's gaze with a challenge of her own.

"Done," he said. "I accept your terms. Speak with Guaa about the warehouse access, and then hurry back with these promised riches, Svetlana Tereshchenko."

~

Svetlana and Indigo followed Guaa into the Unfathomed Enclave's largest warehouse, this one situated on one of the non-floating portions of the archipelago. Based on its sheer size, it was clear why it wasn't on a floating portion—the weight would overwhelm even the strongest of engines or geysers.

Guaa gestured around. "I guess he's given you full access. Give me a few minutes, and I'll bring you someone who knows their way around the place."

Svetlana nodded and looked at Indigo. The boy's eyes were enormous as he took in the vast shelves filled with the various parts Dargon's shipping service had salvaged over the years.

"Too much," Indigo murmured under his breath.

"We'll have a guide soon," Svetlana said, grasping Indigo's shoulders gently and turning him to face her, so his attention was drawn away from the overwhelming amount of stuff. "We're only looking for what we need to fix the diving bell today, okay? We need a new tube to replace the one that melted. We need to make sure the new one isn't going to melt."

"Steel," Indigo said with a nod. "Heavy, but won't melt."

"What about something in between steel and copper?" Svetlana asked. "Wouldn't that be better? Light and not melting?"

Indigo nodded, but his brow was furrowed. "I need Drassilis's brain."

"We can bring Drassilis in to help you," Svetlana said, "but remember we also need to find parts to build a big propeller for Annette."

"With strong housing so no one gets hurt," Indigo agreed.

Guaa and a young woman of Indigo's size and build entered the warehouse. The young woman's hair was a bright purple, her skin a light copper color, and her dark eyes searched Indigo's face, paying no attention to Svetlana.

"Where are you from?" she asked, her voice faint and almost whispery.

"Dougou," Indigo said, staring at the young woman as intently as she regarded him.

The young woman tucked her chin in a bit, as though she was trying to move her eyes away from Indigo. When she spoke again, her voice was louder. "Oh. Okay. I'm April. I work here. What do you need?"

Indigo frowned. "You're not from Dougou."

"No. Never heard of it."

Ticking the elements off on his fingers, Indigo began, "Strong, light, bendable conduit—"

April nodded once and began walking toward the shelves.

Indigo looked at Svetlana, and she gestured for him to follow April. As the two of them walked away, Indigo continued his list of needed parts.

Svetlana looked at Guaa. "Does April know her stuff?"

Guaa shrugged. "She should." Then she turned her gaze to Svetlana. "You're really going to come back and work for Dargon full-time if this plan doesn't work?"

"We don't have much of a choice. The Air Fleet is hot on our heels on this, and we've got—" Svetlana trailed off. She wasn't certain how much she wanted to tell Guaa about the ghosts. If the folks in the Unfathomed Enclave had never been visited by a ghost ship, they might not be inclined to believe what Svetlana and her crew had witnessed. "Well, there are other competitors too."

"Dargon had me send the Air Fleet elsewhere for supplies, so you're one step up on them on that count," Guaa said. "If there are other competitors, I don't think they've been snooping around here."

"That's encouraging," Svetlana said. "How far out do your people patrol?"

Guaa barked out a laugh. "We don't patrol, Captain. We've just got enough traffic coming and going every day that we see plenty, and we haven't seen anything we can't account for here. Just you lot and the Air Fleet."

Svetlana nodded. If the ghosts didn't want to be seen, they wouldn't be. The ghosts could have easily already recovered the treasure, and no one would be the wiser for it. The buoys they'd left to prevent the ghosts from finding the area would only work on a metaphysical level—if the ghosts went to the location and saw the strange devices, they were certain to suspect something—but when it came down to it, Svetlana wasn't sure what else they could do to stop the ghosts.

"You know that when you come back, you're not going to get any special privileges," Guaa said.

Svetlana mustered up a smile. "That assumes we're going to have to come back."

"Well, you're worried about something. I can tell that much."

"You ever gone diving into the boiling seas?" Svetlana asked, arching an eyebrow at Guaa.

Guaa shuddered. "Not personally. That's salvagers' work. I suppose like them, you might not even survive to come back and work for us. I guess we'd better get a location so we can send in salvage."

"Jo will stay with the ship while we dive," Svetlana said. "She'll bring it back to you with whatever crew we've got left."

"You're diving, then?" Guaa asked.

Svetlana nodded. "Back in the old days, they used to talk about captains going down with their ships. Consider this the equivalent, I suppose."

"Who else, then?"

Svetlana considered the options. Jo would need to keep the ship aloft, and she'd need some combination of Indigo, Deliah, and Drassilis to keep the engines running. On top of that, Svetlana wasn't sure either of the kids wanted to go on the dive, and Drassilis had already said he was too large to fit into the diving bell. Since they'd want to keep the doctor topside too, that meant just she and Athos would be going. She turned to Guaa. "Fancy coming with?"

Guaa chuckled. "Not even a little. Someone's got to survive to keep Dargon in line."

CHAPTER TEN

Back on *The Silent Monsoon*, the hold was a flurry of activity. Tubing snaked across the floor, with April joining Indigo to help install the new materials, which both of them had confirmed were made of a lightweight alloy of copper and steel that was not a melting hazard.

Meanwhile, Drassilis worked with Annette on reassembling a pair of large propellers, salvaged from an old turbine somewhere, and connecting them to a driveshaft that could be activated by diverting steam from the engines. The propellers would remain on the ship, one of them responsible for pushing clean air into the diving bell and the other for pulling used air out.

Deliah ran between the two projects, carrying tools and offering occasional suggestions to both teams. When she wasn't running, she worked on repairing a pair of heavy waterproofed canvas suits, which currently hung from one of the rafters of the hold. She had removed the large glass globes from the necks of both of the suits and placed them on the floor below. The globes reflected the hold upside down and warped into a bulbous image.

Svetlana realized what the suits reminded her of—a pair of giant insects that had been decapitated and stripped of their skins. Her own skin crawled, and the fact that she and Athos would have to wear those suits doubled the impact her thoughts had.

Athos and Jo stood back from the chaos with Svetlana. "Sveta," Athos asked, "do you really think this is going to work?"

"I have faith in Annette and Indy," Svetlana said. "I think they both know what they're doing."

"But?" Athos prompted her.

Svetlana shrugged. "We don't know what we're getting into. We could get down there and find out we're stuck inside the diving bell and can't get out to get the treasure. We've got the net, but it's only going to reach so far."

"Yeah, we're relying on a lot of luck to get to the right place," Athos agreed.

"I feel like we're going to wind up just out of reach of the Gem, and then we're going to have to hope the ship can move our position just a little bit."

"We can move you," Jo said. "We're going to get the Gem."

Athos chuckled. "I just can't help but think of the millions of little things that can go wrong."

"What if it goes right?" Jo asked, arching an eyebrow.

Svetlana chuckled. "Jo, I've never seen you so positive."

Jo shrugged. "I could have died. I didn't. You won't either."

"Wish I could be so sure," Athos said.

Jo smiled. "If you die, a witch doctor can bring you back to life."

"Oh, that's comforting," Svetlana said. "Just Athos, right?"

Jo considered for a moment, then pointed at both Athos and Svetlana.

Annette joined the other crew. "What's going on?"

"Speculation about life after death, Doc," Athos said. "How's the construction going?"

"Well enough," Annette said, glancing over her shoulder at the work. "The propellers are going to be a good addition, but they're going to make it difficult for you to communicate with us topside. I've asked Deliah to find some bells, so we can rig those to the pulley system. Then you'll be able to signal us from below. One ring to stop, lots of ringing if you're ready to come back?"

"Doc, you act like you've got this all under control," Svetlana said. "Thank you."

Annette shrugged. "It's not going to be easy, but the best we can do is to be prepared for whatever might come up." She turned to Jo. "You've got the net ready?"

Jo nodded.

"Then I'm going to strongly suggest you don't open the diving bell door if you don't have to, Captain. That's honestly where I anticipate the most things could go wrong."

"And yet, we still have to wear those gods-be-cursed suits?" Athos asked. "They're not right for either of our colorations."

"You sound like Chickie." Annette chuckled. "The suits are a precaution. A backup plan, if you will."

"Noted," Svetlana said, "but I still want them checked over to make sure we *can* venture out of the diving bell. Even if you think we shouldn't."

"I can always hope you won't have to," Annette said.

"And I can always pray some more," Athos suggested. "Sveta, you're gonna have to accept me praying every step of the way."

"I do," Svetlana said. "I just don't know how well the Skyfather's going to hear you underwater."

~

Deliah paused mid-step between the two groups working on the diving bell. "They're here," she said, her voice eerily calm.

Svetlana's gaze snapped to Deliah. "The ghosts?"

Deliah nodded. She kept her gaze trained on the floor, not looking at any of the equipment she had been helping with. She remained standing, rather than convulsing and falling to the floor of the hold. After a long moment of silence, she finally said, "Can't see me. I think."

Drassilis rolled from his position near the propellers toward Deliah. "Are you certain, Deliah?"

Deliah smiled wanly. "They haven't stolen my brain."

"Captain Tereshchenko," Drassilis said, "someone should check the anti-Aether device on the bridge to ensure that it continues to function correctly."

"Jo?" Svetlana asked.

Jo nodded and raced toward the stairs out of the hold.

"What does it feel like?" Indigo asked, having risen from working on the tubing to take Deliah's hand.

"Nothing this time," Deliah said, still not looking around, though she clutched Indigo's hand tightly enough that his fingertips were turning bright pink. "Just knowing."

"If you know they're here," Athos began.

"If the device is working, they shouldn't know she's here at all," Svetlana said.

Drassilis dipped his head in an approximation of a nod and said, "That is correct, Captain Tereshchenko."

"What about the buoys?" Annette asked. "Any way to tell if they're still working?"

"Not unless we inspect them visually," Drassilis said. "Even if we could, they will likely not stop the ghosts from entering the water."

"That's too bad," Athos said. "I'd love to see some ghosts get fried by our anti-Aether net trap thing."

"How much longer until we're ready to go?" Svetlana asked.

Drassilis rotated the upper half of his body toward the diving bell, then back to face Svetlana. "The tubing appears to be mostly complete. We are still working on the air exchange system."

Jo thundered down the stairs and nodded vigorously as soon as her face was in view.

"Good work, everyone," Svetlana said. Turning her attention to Indigo and April, she asked, "Do you think we're ready to test the new tubing?"

Indigo nodded. "We did."

"How?" Athos asked. "The diving bell hasn't moved."

April joined Indigo. "We did a sample test. We boiled water in the tea pan, put in some of the tubing, and it didn't melt."

"The ocean will be in contact with the tubing for some time," Annette said, rising from where she had been working. "Hours, potentially. A few minutes in the tea pan isn't enough of a test."

"That's why it was a sample test," April said. "We didn't want to install all this tubing if boiling tea water would melt it in a few minutes."

"Good thinking, April," Svetlana said. "If the ghosts are in the area, though, we need to move. Just because they can't sense us doesn't mean they can't see us if they fly past."

Annette shook her head. "We have to test the tubing, Captain. If it springs a leak, you'll drown before you get to the treasure."

"Then let's test the tubing now, without hauling the diving bell back into the water again. You and Drassilis can keep working on the propellers. Deliah, are you done with the suits?"

Deliah nodded. "Much as I can be."

"Good enough," Svetlana said. "You help them out too. The rest of us will see if the tubing and the suits are going to work."

~

The bulk of the crew, plus April, hovered near the loading area in the hull, watching the boiling waves lapping against the length of tubing they'd lowered into the water. Beside the tubing, only the glass domes of the suits were partially visible, and the heat of the water surrounding them had fogged up their exteriors enough that no one could tell if they were taking on any water.

Svetlana's attention alternated between the tubing and her pocket watch. Finally, she nodded. "Fifteen minutes. Let's haul it back up."

Indigo and April began hauling in the tubing, while Athos used the pulley system to bring the suits up from the water and back onboard.

"Propellers are done," Annette said, walking over while wiping her hands on a grimy towel. "We've got them connected to the engines for power, which means we're not going to be able to make a very quick getaway."

"Especially because we're going to need to use the gangplank winch to pull the diving bell back up, since Athos is going below with me," Svetlana said. "What I wouldn't give for a second ship."

"Do you think Dargon would loan us one?"

Svetlana grimaced. "I think we're at the limit of our asking favors from Dargon, unless the Last Emperor's Hoard winds up being too much for us to carry in a single trip."

"What about the Kavisolis?" Annette suggested. "We could send an airwave from the Unfathomed Enclave when we drop April off."

Svetlana didn't want to involve Lar and his family with this endeavor, though she also didn't want to admit that to Annette. She trusted the Kavisolis far more than she trusted the Air Fleet, but the potential of the Gem of the Seas was an enormous temptation. While Lar likely wouldn't try to take it for his own, she couldn't be certain that his entire family would see things similarly. So instead, she offered a secondary explanation to Annette. "We don't have enough time to contact anyone else to get a second ship out here."

Nodding, Annette said, "Then the best we can do is be aware we're going to be diverting a lot of power to keeping you and Athos alive and getting you out that way. It's worth it to me."

"I appreciate that," Svetlana said. The entire crew was trying to remain positive about this excursion, but Svetlana knew there was a very real possibility of so many things going wrong. She'd tried to put as many of them out of her mind as she could, but that didn't entirely stop new ones from cropping up at every turn.

The tubing and diving suits had been fully pulled into the hold, dripping warm water onto the floor—their route back to the ship had kept them in the cold air for long enough to cool the remaining ocean water to a reasonable temperature. April, Indigo, and Deliah converged on them, examining both the tubing and the suits while chattering amongst themselves.

Although April hadn't spent much time with the two youngest crew members, she'd taken to working with them quite easily and even started adopting some of their speech patterns. She approached the adult members of the crew. "Tubing is good. Suits have a few small leaks, but they won't take long to patch."

"Hello?" an unidentifiable voice echoed through the hold, emanating from the speaking tube.

"Who's there?" Svetlana asked.

"Bevie," the voice replied. "Dargon sent me. There are a couple of Air Fleet ships inbound, and he thought you should know."

Svetlana ran for the stairs and rushed onto the bridge. Bevie was a small woman, shorter even than Svetlana, with nut-brown skin and close-cropped curls of gold and auburn. She wore a full suit of leathers just a shade darker than her skin and a pair of goggles. Outside the bridge, her propeller bike, a craft sufficient to make the short jaunt between the islands of the Unfathomed Enclave and out to where *The Silent Monsoon* had flown to run the remaining tests, rested against the bulkhead.

"Just a couple of ships?" Svetlana asked.

Bevie nodded. "Two, to be precise. They haven't arrived yet, but they were spotted out near where you lot put those old buoys?"

"Does Dargon have someone out watching that area?" Svetlana asked.

"Naw, but there's enough ships flying to and fro that they spotted the unknown ships—or, rather, not unknown, because Air Fleet's got a bit of a distinctive sail and flag configuration."

Svetlana nodded. "Thanks for the news. Have you heard anything else?"

"Oh, I hear plenty, but not much that's likely to help you," Bevie said.

"Do you need any help launching back to wherever you came from?" Svetlana asked.

Bevie shook her head. "I'm self-sufficient, but thanks for the offer. Be seeing you later." She strode out to reclaim her propeller bicycle, positioned it at the open spot in the bulkhead, and took off a moment later, the power of her legs spinning the propeller that kept the small transport aloft.

Jo joined Svetlana on the bridge in time to watch Bevie take off. The two women watched the bicyclist maneuver through the heavy air currents near the ship, and Jo let out a soft whistle.

Svetlana looked at Jo. "If we have to run our airflow propellers and the ship, do you think we can run the cloud generator at the same time?"

Jo hesitated for a moment, brow furrowed, then nodded. "Three things. But not four."

Realization dawned on Svetlana. "Only three things at once? We can run the propellers, the ship, and the cloud generator, but that would leave out the winch."

Jo nodded again.

Svetlana considered the various permutations possible. The ship had to be aloft, a fact that was not negotiable. If Svetlana wanted it hidden in a cloud as well, that meant they wouldn't be able to pump air through the system while the winch was in use to lower and raise them. While there would be some airflow without the propellers, Annette had felt strongly enough that the propellers were needed that she'd seen to their construction, which meant that they, too, would need to be a constant, leaving the winch and the cloud as the non-essential pieces—except for when the winch was absolutely essential.

"Then there's no easy way to get around it. The ship and propellers stay running, and you'll have to alternate between the cloud generator and the winch. That being said, favor the cloud."

"Because it's from Lar?" Jo joked.

Svetlana bit back an initial protestation and replied, "Because I'd rather the Air Fleet and ghosts can't find us so easily."

CHAPTER ELEVEN

Svetlana chuckled when Athos stomped back into the hold, wearing a bulky and uncomfortable protective suit identical to the one she wore. She'd had a brief amount of time to make peace with her suit. Movement made her feel more awkward than she had when bundled up in the snow at Orwall. Stomping was, in fact, the easiest way of walking, and the heavy boots just added to that. She could only ball her hands into fists, not really do anything with her fingers in the heavily padded gloves. And between the streaked glass of the helmet and her eyepatch, since her monocular required occasional adjustment when she wore it, her vision was half of what it normally was, at best.

Annette stopped Athos and began her checks of his suit, as she had done for Svetlana. Athos grumbled faintly the entire time, possibly saying things Annette could hear, but the suits muffled both the volume of their voices and their hearing, so Svetlana only heard Athos's complaints as a soft rumble.

Finally, Annette gave Athos a smile and a raised thumb, and Athos continued stomping over to Svetlana.

"I hate this," he said, just clearly enough for her to hear when they stood side by side.

"Me too," Svetlana replied. "Just remember. Treasure."

"Not as much as we could have had."

"I'd rather be alive than richer."

Athos rolled his eyes, but then nodded. "After you, Captain."

Svetlana approached the diving bell and ducked in order to get through the door. The helmet of her suit barely fit through the doorframe. Once inside, she sat on a small stool that was bolted to the floor. But as Athos tried to step inside, he kicked her knees.

"You're going to have to wait to sit until after Athos gets in," Annette shouted from outside the diving bell.

Svetlana rose and pressed her back against the wall of the diving bell, giving Athos enough room to maneuver himself inside. They moved around each other, almost like a dance, in order to find enough space for each of them to be fully inside the diving bell and comfortable.

Annette poked her head through the door and grinned. "Alright, we're going to seal you up tight now, and then Drassilis will get you moved into position for the drop."

"You only smile because you don't have to do this," Athos said.

"You'll be fine," Annette continued, as though she hadn't been interrupted. "Just remember. Your suits have valves built in so you can breathe normally, but if you don't have to leave the diving bell, stay in. Got it?"

Svetlana nodded, and assumed Athos did the same, as Annette retreated from the doorway and closed the outer door to the diving bell. Looking for the inner door, Svetlana found only the remaining hinges. As she tried to imagine how much more cramped the space would be if the door remained, the diving bell lurched, and she fumbled for Athos's gloved hands.

She found them, but Athos gently batted her hands away. She shifted slightly to see his hands, and found them palms up, as if in prayer.

Svetlana wasn't one for praying. She occasionally swore on the Skyfather's name or made half-hearted pleas to his mercy, but she wasn't really a believer in some unseen lord of the air. Athos, however, was more devout in his beliefs, and the two of them had a long-standing mutual understanding that he wouldn't try to get her to believe, while she wouldn't try to convince him the Skyfather was only a legend.

In a position such as this, though, she couldn't help but wonder if maybe a little prayer wouldn't hurt. She placed her hands in a similar position to Athos's, flanking his on both sides. Though their gloves prevented them from feeling much with their hands, the presence of Athos's hands between hers was comforting, and she hoped her hands offered the same support to him.

Then the diving bell swung from side to side, suspended in the open air outside of the hull of *The Silent Monsoon*, equal parts exhilarating and dizzying.

"Here we go," Athos said.

~

The cooling coils between the two layers of the diving bell obscured much of the pair of small windows, and the glass of the windows themselves was thick. Between that, the helmet, and Svetlana's blind eye, she couldn't really see what was happening outside of the diving bell. Their descent was slow, but there was nothing else to look at other than Athos's slightly obscured face, so Svetlana stood and looked out the nearer of the two windows.

The water surrounding them was dark, closer to black than blue or gray. The small lantern they had inside the diving bell barely penetrated outside of their capsule, but it apparently shone enough to attract a few denizens of the deep.

The first time something bumped up against the window, it took all Svetlana's willpower to not scream. The creature outside was longer than it was wide and covered in silvery barbed scales.

"How do things live in a boiling ocean?" she asked, more to herself than to Athos.

"Adaptation," Athos replied. "People still fish, and the fish aren't already cooked when they're caught."

Svetlana chuckled. "Stubborn, like us."

"Or foolhardy. Don't rule that out."

Another sea creature moved into view, this one with translucent tentacles that reddened as they pulsated. One of the tentacles latched on to the window with a row of small suction cups, and the tip of its tentacle wormed around the edges of the glass.

"We're sealed up tight, right?" Athos asked, clearly watching the window Svetlana was looking at.

Svetlana nodded, watching the tentacled creature with mute horror. Her heartbeat pounded in her ears, and she tried to calm herself. Before she was able to get her breathing under control, the tentacle detached from the window, and the creature swam away in search of more accessible food, or so Svetlana wanted to believe.

"Sealed tight. Maybe we'll bring back things to sell the scientists on the outside," Svetlana said.

"As long as they don't find their way inside."

Svetlana turned her attention back to Athos. "We might have to go outside for the Gem. If we find other things, we'll have to strap them on the outside."

"You think we can walk around out there?"

"We've got these suits," Svetlana said, gesturing to the awkward thing she wore.

Athos laughed nervously. "Don't trust them as far as I can throw them."

"Annette says they're watertight."

"Are they crushing depths of the ocean and *boiling* watertight?"

"I'm hoping sea caves means no water," Svetlana said.

"We can only hope," Athos said. "What if we can't go out?"

"Then we have to go back up and back down and hope we get a better second landing. Or third. Or tenth."

Athos chuckled. "So delightful."

~

The diving bell settled with a soft thud, which startled both Svetlana and Athos.

"Is that it? Are we here?" Svetlana asked, rising to look out the window.

Outside, a faint glow illuminated a nearby rock formation. Searching for the source of the light, all Svetlana saw was some sort of bioluminescent lichen growing on the rock, unlike anything she had seen before. A faint gasp escaped her lips, certainly not loud enough for Athos to hear.

A series of thumps on the roof of the diving bell turned her gasp into a more panicked sound. "Tubing." She reached up to the ceiling and tugged the string that would ring the bell back on the ship once. She couldn't hear the bell through the long expanse of tubing, but when the thumping stopped soon after, she assumed her message had been successfully received.

"It's beautiful out there," Svetlana said, returning to peer out the small window.

"I can't see it," Athos said.

Svetlana maneuvered around the inside of the diving bell to give Athos access to the window she had been looking through, and looked out the other window, which faced into the darkness of the boiling ocean.

"Dry on this side," Athos said. "I think it's an air pocket."

"Will the water rush in if we open the door?" Svetlana asked.

"I guess we get to find out."

Svetlana approached the door, then turned to face Athos again. "Just in case—" she began.

Athos shook his head inside his helmet, holding up one gloved hand. "No last words. We're going to be fine."

With a small nod, Svetlana turned back to the wheel that would open the door to the diving bell. She cranked it until she heard a faint escape of air, and then began turning it more slowly, watching the seal around the door. A rivulet of water crept in, and she paused. "We've got a leak."

"See if it gets worse?" Athos asked. His pressure-suited arm reached past Svetlana and a gloved finger diverted the rivulet. "It's not hot."

Svetlana moved the wheel another notch, all the while watching for further drips entering the diving bell. Another hiss of air made her pause, but the leaking didn't increase. She gave the wheel another half turn, and it stopped, having reached the point at which it was fully disengaged.

When she pushed on the door, it swung open as it would have on dry land, as though the air and pressure were no different than on a platform city or an island. She waited a moment for the inevitable rush of water, but none came. Hesitantly, she took a step out of the diving bell.

"It's dry out there," Athos said, wonder apparent in his voice. He chuckled. "Jo got us in the exact right spot."

"She can't hear you," Svetlana said, taking a few more steps outside of the diving bell. "And it was everyone. Not just Jo."

"Yeah, but she has the most charmed life of us all."

"Except for getting sent to jail, and having her jaw broken. Twice." Svetlana looked around the dry space, far beneath the waves, now that she was a few feet ahead of the diving bell. If she turned around, she could see the roiling water, but something prevented it from breaching this space. She approached the water, good eye wide, trying to spot whatever was keeping it out.

"Careful, Sveta," Athos said as he emerged from the diving bell. "Don't pop the bubble."

Svetlana took a deep, shuddering breath as she stepped away from the dividing line between water and dry cave and nodded. "Think the treasure wound up in here? None of this makes sense."

Athos nodded in agreement. "But it's true. Underwater, and there's air, or we'd be gasping. Maybe it's natural? Maybe it's magic. Let's not poke it. We're not scientists."

"Wish we were," Svetlana said. She took a moment to get a better impression of the cave they'd entered. The rock formations looked natural to her untrained eye, filled with crags and outcroppings common to caves. The glowing lichen was patchy across the walls, but it provided enough light that they could tell this part of the sea cave was devoid of any treasure. "We should map this, write down our observations—"

"Can't write in these gloves," Athos replied. "Also, no paper or pencils."

Svetlana nodded, her curiosity unabated. "Annette is going to be so upset she missed this. Can you imagine how many people would kill to be here?"

Athos dropped a heavy gloved hand on Svetlana's shoulder and turned her to face him. "I get it, but we don't know how long we've got to find the treasure. So let's get moving. If it works, maybe we'll make another trip later."

"Alright," Svetlana agreed. "I'm keeping my eye open for the shiny stuff."

CHAPTER TWELVE

The last thing Svetlana and Athos expected to find in the sea caves was other living people.

Svetlana immediately amended that to other semi-living people when she realized they were all slightly translucent, in shades of grays, and dressed like they'd come from a costume party or, perhaps, another time.

"Ghosts," Athos said. "They got here before us."

"Yeah, but no treasure," Svetlana said. She glanced at Athos, who was fumbling at his hip for a weapon. "We don't have guns. They don't work on ghosts anyway."

"You're being far too rational, Sveta," Athos said.

With a shrug, Svetlana said, "As long as they don't attack us, we'll be fine."

A group of five ghosts made their way in Svetlana and Athos's direction. The one in the lead, a man wearing the sort of frilly clothing and hat that placed him a good hundred years removed from his time period of origin, squinted at Svetlana. "Don't I know you?" he asked, his voice ragged.

Svetlana shrugged. "Did you kidnap a scientist from her house a few months back?"

Recognition dawned on the man's face. "Ah, yes, you're the living one who tried to save her."

"She managed to escape your grasp anyway," Svetlana said, grinning. "Here for the treasure?"

"Same as you, I suppose," the ghost said, looking over Svetlana and Athos, "but you're at a disadvantage here, what with you being weaponless, and us being armed."

The group of ghosts moved closer to Svetlana and Athos, brandishing or drawing weapons as they approached.

"Great," Athos said. "Just what we didn't want."

Svetlana held up her hands. "We don't want to fight. We're here for one thing."

"I suspect we're here for the same thing," the ghost replied, still moving forward with menace glinting in his eyes. "We've been told not to let you get it."

"Told?" Svetlana asked. "By who?"

"Me." A woman's voice, clear enough that even Svetlana's helmet didn't muffle it, rang out.

Svetlana searched for the source. It had sounded like ...

Then she saw her. Lady Elinor de Whittvy stood atop a rock outcropping a dozen meters away. Her hair was no longer as bright as it once was, and her pink shirt had faded to a grayish-pink. Her pale skin was blindingly white in her generally grayed-out palette, making her look even more delicate and fragile than she had before. The faded coloration suited her, and the lady scientist was just as beautiful as she'd been when Svetlana first met her.

And just like that, her appearance confirmed what Svetlana had known, instinctively, but not quite accepted without seeing it with her own eyes. Lady de Whittvy had died from the gunshot wound on Bonebriar, and she'd become a part of the ghost ship's crew.

Svetlana finally found her voice. "You're ... I suppose you're not alive, but you're still in existence?"

Lady de Whittvy smiled. "You could say that." Tilting her head to the side, she asked, "Did you miss me?"

"More than you could imagine," Svetlana said, the words rushing out before she could stop them. She didn't elaborate on the reasons why she had missed Lady de Whittvy, largely related to her potential knowledge about the casks of Cranglimmering and the map they contained, but also because she found the noblewoman attractive and intriguing. "We have—well, had, now—so many questions, but I guess we're in the right spot."

"Yes, you are, I suppose. We found your little beacons."

"Beacons?" Svetlana asked, her brow furrowing.

"Oh, I suppose they were meant to keep us away, but they didn't quite work that way. The buoys, with the devices. After all, they were my idea—" Lady de Whittvy trailed off and then gasped. "You got Drassilis running?"

Svetlana nodded. "Indy did. Well, Indy and Deliah. She's been working for you, hasn't she?"

Lady de Whittvy shrugged. "I needed some way of keeping tabs on you. Don't worry, I won't hurt the girl. Really, I don't want to hurt any of you. I just want the Gem."

Svetlana glanced at Athos. He held both of his hands up in surrender, but his gaze wasn't on Lady de Whittvy or Svetlana. He was watching the ghosts in front of him, weapons still drawn, who were watching the conversation between the two women. He'd edged closer to the nearest of the ghosts, likely with disarming the ghost in mind. Svetlana wanted to signal him to wait, but he wasn't paying any attention to her at the moment.

"We're here for the Gem too," Svetlana said, "as you might have already gathered. We know what will happen if it's used—"

"As do I, Sveta dear." Lady de Whittvy smiled. "It's only logical, after all. If the seas stop boiling, everything goes back to the way it was before. No more Republic."

Svetlana fixed Lady de Whittvy's gaze with her own. "That means no more platform cities. Thousands of people drowned, as their homes plummet into the ocean. You can't use the Gem right away. People need time to move to safety."

Lady de Whittvy nodded slowly, but then pursed her lips. "Do you realized the level of endeavor you're proposing?"

"Yes," Svetlana said. She glanced at the ghosts. Most of them had lowered their weapons, or at least weren't brandishing them in a way that made her fear they might attack if she moved closer to Lady de Whittvy. So she took a tentative step forward. "The Republic should be stopped, but we need a plan. We can't just stop everything at once."

"I suppose you're right," Lady de Whittvy said, pouting. "It's a shame there aren't any instructions for the Gem of the Seas about just making parts of the ocean stop boiling. You know, a quick show of power to convince the Republic we're not bluffing?"

Svetlana had to force herself not to chuckle. "Yes, a shame, but we can't be sure it works like that."

Lady de Whittvy's gaze snapped to Svetlana, and she held out a hand. Svetlana froze, only lifting her hands in a gesture of surrender. "You may not be sure, but I have it on good authority that it does work. Captain Windlass assures me."

"Windlass?" Svetlana asked. "Should I know that name?"

Someone joined Lady de Whittvy on the rock outcropping, a man who had likely possessed dark hair and skin in life, but now looked grayed and faded like Lady de Whittvy did. His clothing, though dim, had the appearance of something that had once cost a lot of money, decorated with unnecessary buttons and beadwork, and his bearing also suggested a noble upbringing. "Captain Windlass, at your service," he said, giving a half-bow.

"Windlass?" Athos said. "How?"

Svetlana looked at Athos. "You know him?"

"Know of," Athos said. "He died—was executed, that is—before I was born. My family is connected to his. We don't talk about it."

"Nobility, then?"

"Former High Councilor. Distant uncle, I guess."

Svetlana nodded and turned her attention back to Lady de Whittvy and the captain of the ghost ship. "Captain Svetlana Tereshchenko of *The Silent Monsoon*," she said, returning his half-bow. "You know how the Gem of the Seas works?"

Captain Windlass nodded. "Pulls the platform cities right out of the air, is what it does."

Svetlana frowned. "That's what I'm trying to stop."

"And in my day, that's exactly what I was trying to make happen. If it hadn't been for Longhurst."

Svetlana blinked a few times, parsing what Captain Windlass had said. "I'm sorry, did you say Longhurst?"

"Aye."

Athos sidled closer to Svetlana, his brow creasing. "What? What's wrong?"

"Longhurst," she said, then drew it out. "Long cursed. The map. It's not cursed at all, is it? It's the Longhurst Map."

"Clever girl," Captain Windlass said, chuckling hoarsely. "Named after High Councilor Emmeline Longhurst. Also dead. Didn't care to join us as a ghost."

"This is somehow relevant to the Gem?" Svetlana asked.

"In a roundabout way. She's the one who put together the map to find where the Last Emperor's fleet crash-landed. But when she came to the same conclusion as you about the platform cities, she was aghast. She was also too proud to destroy her work, so instead she hid the map in the Cranglimmering casks." Captain Windlass drew his lips into a tight line. "And that's why she had to die."

"You killed her, didn't you?" Athos asked. "Killed her, took her estate, got executed for it?"

"You know your history, then," Captain Windlass said.

"Bits and pieces," Athos said. "But I agree with Lady Longhurst and my captain. The Gem of the Seas needs to be kept out of the wrong hands. Like yours."

"Not yet," Lady de Whittvy said, a fierce edge to her voice that hadn't been there before. "It hasn't fallen into anyone's hands yet." She turned her attention to Svetlana. "You want me to wait before dropping the platform cities into the ocean. What have they ever done for you, Captain Tereshchenko?"

"Plenty," Svetlana spat back. "Everyone uses platform cities. The High Council. The Air Fleet."

Lady de Whittvy shrugged, her gaze somewhere in the distance as though she was bored with this conversation. "Neither of those parties are particularly compelling to me."

"It doesn't matter," Svetlana said. "There are thousands of people who will die."

"People die all the time. Do you truly believe your hands are clean?"

Svetlana shook her head. "They're not, but that doesn't give us the right to condemn innocent people to their deaths, just to get back at the Republic."

Lady de Whittvy shared a look with Captain Windlass, and murmured something too quietly for Svetlana to hear, especially through her helmet. The ghostly captain retreated from the rock outcropping, and Lady de Whittvy followed him. But he continued deeper into the sea caves, while Lady de Whittvy approached Svetlana and Athos.

"Svetlana—Sveta—" Lady de Whittvy began. She reached a hand toward the side of Svetlana's helmet, then paused and pinned Athos beneath her gaze. "Could you give me a few minutes alone with your captain?"

Athos inhaled sharply. "Sveta?"

Svetlana looked at Lady de Whittvy for a moment. Death had changed her. Perhaps she'd always had this ruthless streak, but Svetlana had never seen it when Lady de Whittvy was alive. She wasn't sure the noblewoman could be trusted anymore, but Svetlana was still intrigued, and she wanted to hear what Lady de Whittvy had to say.

She turned to Athos and jerked her head sharply to the side. The two of them retreated slightly from Lady de Whittvy.

"I don't like it," Athos said, his gloved hands clenched into fists. "Windlass is a murderer. He killed Longhurst, *personally*, because she wouldn't help him find the Gem of the Seas. The ghosts have known about this for years. Now they're here with your dead girlfriend saying, 'we can talk about this.' This whole thing is fishier than this ocean."

Svetlana nodded. "I don't like it either. She's not my girlfriend, dead or alive, but I want to talk to her. You can keep looking for the Gem."

Athos shook his head. "I'm not getting too far away from you. They're ghosts. They can probably breathe underwater. We can't. We've only got one way out of here."

"I'll make it quick," Svetlana agreed, "and we won't go far."

Athos nodded, though worry still shone in his eyes. "Very quick. They've got more eyes looking for this than us."

Svetlana nodded and returned to Lady de Whittvy. "Athos will stay over there. What is it?"

Lady de Whittvy smiled. "Well, for one, I wanted to tell you that if you feel any guilt at all for my current state, you should stop."

"You wouldn't be dead if you hadn't been standing beside me when Narci's troops got trigger happy."

"That's in the past, Sveta, and to be perfectly honest, being a ghost is freeing. I can work in my lab for hours without those annoying human needs."

"That's great," Svetlana said, forcing a wan smile to her lips. "Now, about the Gem—"

"You're absolutely right, you know. Making the Republic give us what we want is critical. If we were to drop the platform cities at once, we won't get what we want out of them. We can try just picking one." She paused. "Perhaps you could get Rrusadon to evacuate, and we'll start there?"

Svetlana tensed. Regardless of the current state of her relationship with Lar, choosing any platform city to use as an example was a decision fraught with difficulties. "That's ... no. Find a different way to show you have the power. You can't get people to give up their homes as a statement. Would you ask the people of Bonebriar to abandon their homes?"

"If it was the only choice, I would in a heartbeat," Lady de Whittvy said. "They'd do as I asked, too."

"The people of Rrusadon might not agree," Svetlana said. "Anyway, I haven't talked to Lar in a while."

"Haven't you?" Lady de Whittvy said, moving a step closer to Svetlana and taking her gloved hand. "Well that is a shame. Would you like to talk about it?"

Lady de Whittvy's hand on Svetlana's glove was cold, but she could feel the slight pressure, too. It distracted her from the question. "You can still touch things?"

"Oh yes," Lady de Whittvy said, leaning closer to Svetlana. "Ghosts are just a different state of being. I'm doing all sorts of research on it. Quite productive so far."

"I'm glad it's not all bad, then," Svetlana said, then shook her head to clear it. "We can talk about that later. Are we agreed that the Gem of the Seas must be handled responsibly, and we can't make an example of a platform city just to prove its power?"

"It's 'we' now, is it?" Lady de Whittvy cooed, taking Svetlana's other hand. "I'm glad for that, Sveta dear."

Svetlana didn't know if Lady de Whittvy still smelled of intoxicating lilac, and in that moment, she was very thankful for the huge bulky suit and helmet. The air passing through the valves on the suit was devoid of any scents, allowing her to keep her wits about her. "I meant in the sense of our agreement."

"Oh," Lady de Whittvy said with a slight pout. "Well, I certainly won't use the Gem of the Seas to do anything until I've made the Republic well aware that it's in my possession, and I have the knowledge to use it. Will you agree to the same, in the event that you find it first?"

"Yes," Svetlana said. "That's a good start. Now—"

"Lady de Whittvy," a strident voice called. "We found it."

CHAPTER THIRTEEN

One of the ghosts held up something resembling a crystal tiara. Some of the crystals were jagged along the edges, looking more like salt than any gemstone, cloudy and plain. In the center of the tiara was a clear piece, smoother and less cloudy than the others surrounding it. Though the bioluminescent lichen didn't cast enough light to refract through the central crystal, it gleamed with its own intensity. It looked so simple, but there was no doubt about it. The ghost held the Gem of the Seas.

"Yes," Lady de Whittvy breathed, releasing Svetlana's hands and surging toward the ghost, her feet not even touching the ground.

Svetlana chased after Lady de Whittvy and heard Athos's footfalls behind her.

"Sveta," Athos called out, tension clear in his voice.

Lady de Whittvy reached the ghost and took the tiara in one hand. With the other, she reached within her skirt and produced a small pistol-like device, which she aimed toward the ceiling. "Sveta, go," she said, her voice cold.

"Bring us with you," Svetlana said, still running toward the ghosts.

For a moment, Lady de Whittvy looked at Svetlana with an expression of sadness, and Svetlana thought a glimmer of hope hidden within. But then Lady de Whittvy spoke. "I can't." She shook her head and pulled the trigger.

At first, the pistol appeared to have no effect. Lady de Whittvy calmly tucked it back into the folds of her skirt, no longer making eye contact with Svetlana.

Then, all around them came the sound of rushing water. In the distance, far beyond the ghosts, an enormous wave crashed through the sea cave, filling the previously dry space.

"Goodbye, Sveta," Lady de Whittvy said, and she and the ghost who had brought her the Gem of the Seas both sped toward the approaching wave.

Svetlana backpedaled a few steps toward where she had left Athos before turning and breaking into as much of a run as she could manage in her unwieldy suit.

Athos's face beneath his helmet was deathly pale, and his eyes were enormous. He fumbled at the front of his suit. "Valves," he shouted. "Close the valves and hold your breath!"

Svetlana slapped at the valves on her own suit, but the gloves didn't give her enough manual dexterity to manipulate the small pieces of mesh and leather on the outside of her suit. On the inside, though ...

She extracted her right arm from the sleeve of her suit, pulling it in toward her torso. The arm of the suit flailed as she wiggled around in the tight space, but she managed to get her right hand to the valves on the inside of the suit. "Pull your arm in," she shouted to Athos. "Run for the diving bell, and close the valves at the last possible moment!"

Running with one arm crushed against her body was difficult, but the adrenaline caused by the ever-loudening waves behind her spurred her forward.

Athos ran as well, the right arm of his suit soon flopping uselessly beside him as he followed Svetlana's instructions.

Behind their diving bell, the wall of water still held. Whatever Lady de Whittvy had done to the far side of the sea caves hadn't reached this far yet, but Svetlana didn't want to find out what would happen if it reached them before they'd sealed up the diving bell.

An uneven patch on the floor of the sea cave surprised Svetlana, and she pitched forward, slamming her helmeted head against the ground.

"Sveta!" Athos shrieked.

Svetlana blinked a few times, jarred by the sudden impact. It felt like gravity had suddenly become stronger than ever. Cracks spiderwebbed across the glass of her helmet. She tried to rise, but her limbs wouldn't cooperate. She needed the leverage of both her arms, and her right arm was still tucked into her suit. She tried to wriggle it back into the sleeve, but her hand couldn't find the arm hole.

And then something swept her torso up from the ground. Her feet still dragged the surface of the sea cave, but she was moving again, more slowly than before. The waves were still behind her, frothing and foaming as they careened off the walls of the sea caves.

Her helmet thumped against something, and then her back hit something else. All around her was gray, smooth, metal. The diving bell.

Athos moved into her field of vision, his legs tangled with hers as he pulled the door shut. He began to crank the wheel with his left arm, then grunted. "Sveta, I need your help."

Svetlana pushed against the metal with her left arm and feet, but only succeeded in kicking Athos several times.

He paused in turning the wheel and reached his left arm to her. She grasped it, and he pulled her to her feet, both of them suffering several kicks to the shins in the process. Without a word, he placed her hand on the wheel, made sure she was standing on her own accord, and then began cranking the wheel again.

Svetlana helped Athos with the wheel, though it felt like her motions did nothing. "The bell," she muttered, looking up at the ceiling and the cord hanging there for them to pull when they wanted to be retrieved.

"We need. The door. Closed. First," Athos said, grunts between his phrases.

Svetlana returned her attention to the wheel, trying not to look past Athos at the waves growing ever closer. Finally, the wheel stopped, and Athos reached up to ring the bell.

Time stretched out interminably before the diving bell began to rise, pushed higher by a surge of waves from the sea caves.

~

Svetlana's grogginess cleared on the journey back to *The Silent Monsoon*, and by the time the diving bell was back in the cargo hold, she was ready to be flying again rather than underwater.

Annette was waiting for them when they came out of the diving bell. Her eyes widened when she saw Svetlana's cracked helmet. "Are you alright?"

Svetlana nodded, removing the helmet. "I fell, running away from a wave. I'll explain later. Have you seen the ghost ship?"

"Not exactly," Annette said as she helped Svetlana begin to remove the rest of her diving suit. "Jo thought she saw something strange in the water, but we couldn't tell what it was. Might have been ghosts."

Drassilis's voice came from the speaking tube. "Doctor Campbell, Jo requests the captain and Athos to come up immediately on their return."

"We're here, Drassilis," Svetlana called back. "Just getting out of these abominable suits."

"Jo is rolling her hands over one another," Drassilis reported. "Ah, she says, 'faster'."

Svetlana wriggled away from Annette's assistance. "We can take these off on the bridge." She tried to run toward the stairs out of the hold, but the suit remained clunky and difficult to maneuver in, perhaps even more so now that she was holding the top half bunched at her waist and still wearing the lower half with its heavy boots. She paused at the bottom of the stairs to finish removing the suit.

Athos had removed his helmet but still wore his suit fully, and he pushed past her and headed up, Annette in his wake.

As soon as her suit was a pile of heavy fabric and metal on the floor of the cargo hold, Svetlana made her way to the bridge.

Drassilis and Jo were positioned at the flying controls, while Athos was at the prow of the ship with the spyglass, and Annette looked back and forth nervously. The ship was surrounded by a fluffy veil of steam, as the cloud generator whirred slightly to maintain the camouflage.

"Air Fleet," Annette said. "Athos is trying to identify the ship."

"Ships," Athos said as he returned from the prow. "There's three of them. No flagship."

"As long as they don't try to come through this cloud, they're not going to spot us, right?" Svetlana asked. "And the ghosts have the Gem, so there's nothing here for the Fleet to find."

"Yes, as long as they don't stumble across us," Athos said.

Svetlana nodded. "Our priority needs to be finding the ghosts. I don't know if Lady de Whittvy is really going to do as she promised or not."

"Mother?" Drassilis asked, his voice almost coming out as a gasp.

"What's going on?" Jo asked, throwing her hands up in a gesture of confusion.

"Right, I guess we need to start from the beginning?" Svetlana asked.

"Just the good parts, at least," Annette said. "You've mentioned the Gem and Vertiline—er, Lady de Whittvy now? Those both seem important."

"Yes, Captain Tereshchenko," Drassilis chimed in. "You said Mother was dead."

"She was. Still is. She's with the ghosts now, as Athos suspected. The sea caves were real, the Gem was there, and her people found it. Then they collapsed whatever magic was keeping the air in the sea caves and took off with the Gem. That's when I cracked my helmet, and Athos saved my life." Svetlana smiled at Athos. "Thank you, by the way."

"Couldn't have you dying," Athos said.

Annette frowned and looked away from Svetlana, and Svetlana followed her gaze. One of the Air Fleet ships was nearing them, and it was on a collision trajectory with *The Silent Monsoon*.

"Right, we need to move." Svetlana turned to Drassilis. "Might I take a turn at the wheel?"

Drassilis moved away from the controls, and Svetlana moved into his place beside Jo. Together, they released the locks on the wheels and began to move out of the Air Fleet ship's path.

The ship moved slowly, the steam cloud still surrounding it. But as they began moving, the Air Fleet ship continued to track the location of the ship, still moving directly toward it.

"They're on to us," Athos said, watching the other ship from the port windows.

"Then our choices are to turn and face them or get out of here," Svetlana said. "I'm a fan of the latter, as we can't beat them for firepower."

Jo nodded and added some speed to their departure. Fragments of the steam cloud trailed off behind them, revealing portions of the ship now that they were moving more quickly. And still the Air Fleet ship tracked them.

"They're pursuing," Athos confirmed.

"Thoughts?" Svetlana asked.

Jo pointed out the windscreen to a naturally occurring bank of clouds.

Svetlana nodded. "That's a good start. Lose them there." She and Jo maneuvered the ship toward the clouds, and the Air Fleet ship changed its trajectory as well.

Athos moved to stand near the cloud generator. "Did we ever find out what the button does?"

Svetlana shook her head. "I haven't spoken to any of the Kavisolis since we left Rrusadon, and I didn't get around to asking Lar about it then."

"Wanna find out?" Athos asked with an impish grin.

"Element of surprise, I suppose," Svetlana said. "Push it."

Athos bent to push the button.

The impact was immediate. *The Silent Monsoon* plummeted, now surrounded by a thick cloud of steam and possibly a bit of smoke. The engines whined, and the ship's forward momentum slowed dramatically.

"What in the—" Svetlana began, but didn't finish her thought as *The Silent Monsoon* leveled out, and the Air Fleet ship shot ahead, far above them.

"Sudden drop, quick stop," Athos barked out with a laugh. "And a really big cloud."

Deliah's voice came through the speaking tube, shakily. "Captain?"

"Are you and Indy alright?" Svetlana asked.

"We're okay. What happened?"

"Tell Indy we found out what the cloud generator button does."

~

The Silent Monsoon flew slowly at their lowered altitude, maneuvering away from the location of the now-flooded sea caves. Indigo came up to the bridge soon after they made their escape from the Air Fleet.

"Button depletes the steam reserves," he said, frowning in the direction of the cloud generator.

Jo chuckled softly. "Makes sense. No speed."

Indigo nodded.

"How long till we can build up a reserve again?" Svetlana asked.

"Hour or two," Indigo said. "Maybe shorter if we turn off the cloud."

Svetlana scanned the skies around the ship and nodded. "I think we're clear of the Air Fleet. May as well turn it off."

Indigo switched the machine off and then headed toward the engine room. Before he reached the stairs, he froze, pointed out the rear window of the bridge, and said, "Ghost ship."

The rest of the crew turned to face the direction he was pointing. In the distance, the ghost ship shimmered in the late afternoon sunlight.

"Why would she be showing herself now?" Svetlana wondered aloud. "Why not stay hidden?"

Drassilis hummed. "Though I have not had the opportunity to fully study the capabilities of such a craft, perhaps it, too, is limited in its ability to remain hidden?"

"Like it lost its steam reserves?" Athos asked.

"Precisely," Drassilis said.

"Hey, Indy, where's that gun you made?" Athos asked.

"Gun?" Svetlana asked. "What gun?"

Indigo hurried down the stairs, then immediately returned carrying a pile of parts tied together with scraps of fabric. If she squinted at it just right, Svetlana could almost make out the vague shape of a gun. It looked like it was made from similar parts to the ones they'd acquired to make the anti-Aether devices, just configured differently. Indigo handed the construct to Athos.

Athos grinned and headed out on deck. Svetlana locked her steering controls and joined him, with Indigo by her side.

"What is that thing?" she asked.

"Anti-Aether gun," Indigo replied. "Like the buoys and the thing that hides the ship from them."

"And I'm going to see if I can shoot them with it," Athos said. "Ask Jo to get us a little closer?"

"Are you sure we want that? Wouldn't it be better to just follow them to wherever they go?"

"Maybe," Athos said, "but after that whole debacle in the sea caves, I'd really love to just get one good shot at them."

With a chuckle, Svetlana said, "I don't disagree. But shooting them out of the sky isn't going to get the Gem back."

Athos grumbled as he lowered the makeshift weapon. "You're not wrong, but do you have to be so right, Sveta?"

"I try," she shot back before ducking back onto the bridge. "Jo, follow the ghost ship."

Jo nodded and released both of the steering columns so she could maneuver the ship. She caught Svetlana's good eye and gestured at the cloud generator, her eyebrows raised in a questioning expression.

"We're already hidden from them with the anti-Aether device, I think," Svetlana said. "Let's build up the steam reserves in case we need more cloud cover later."

The Silent Monsoon's reduced speed at the moment was considerably slower than most airships. The ghost ship didn't appear to be traveling at a high speed either, but with their paces evenly matched, there was no chance of the *Monsoon* catching up to the ghost ship.

Svetlana studied the gauges on the control panel, tapping at the one indicating their speed. "If we could just get a little bit more speed, we'd give them a good chase."

Jo shook her head enough that Svetlana caught a glimpse of the motion, even with Jo on her bad eye's side.

Turning to face Jo, Svetlana asked. "No more speed?"

Jo shook her head again, then shrugged.

"Nothing to be done for it," Svetlana said, interpreting Jo's movements, which earned her a nod from Jo.

Out on deck, Athos began growling curses. Svetlana turned to look at him. The ghost ship no longer hovered in front of their ship.

"It went back into Aetherwhere," Athos snarled, handing the anti-Aether gun back to Indigo and stomping across the deck toward the bridge.

Svetlana stepped aside to let Athos and Indigo past. "Do you think we can estimate their trajectory?"

"We could try," Athos said, "but I really don't know a thing about how trajectories work in Aetherwhere."

Svetlana moved to the map on the bridge. "Drassilis, what's our heading?"

"South by southeast, Captain."

Svetlana traced a line across the map, her fingers not coming across any likely locales. "Well, I see three possibilities. One, they're going to look for some other treasure we don't know about."

"We could fill books with what we don't know about ghosts," Athos said, chuckling softly. "And treasures."

Svetlana continued. "Two, they're planning to change course while they're in Aetherwhere."

Behind them, Jo rapped her knuckles on the steering column. When Svetlana and Athos turned toward her, she nodded.

"If we had the ability to slip in and out of Aetherwhere like that, I think Jo would have made doing so an art form," Svetlana said.

Jo grinned broadly at that.

Svetlana continued. "Which leads us to the third possibility: them having a secret hidden base in the middle of nowhere. Which gets us about as far as either of the other two options get us."

CHAPTER FOURTEEN

"So how do we find something we can't see?" Svetlana asked.

Athos nodded, deep in thought. "I mean, we've found things we can't see plenty of times before, but somehow 'in Aetherwhere' seems a little more extreme than just something we can't see."

Svetlana echoed his thoughtful nod. "Drassilis, how much do you know about how Lady—er, Dr. Dowhty—constructed her 'back ways' to her lab?"

"Unfortunately, very little," Drassilis admitted. "She constructed that portion of her home before she created me, and it was not accessible to me."

"Is there anything she ever told you about the theory behind it, or anything like that?"

"No, Captain Tereshchenko, I am afraid she did not. The only thing she told me is it might not be entirely compatible with my composition, so it was best if I stay far from that portion of the house."

Svetlana arched her eyebrow. "Not entirely compatible with your composition? That suddenly sounds suspicious."

"Sort of, but she also had Drassilis help work on this anti-Aether device that we've now replicated." Athos gestured at the unit that ostensibly prevented the ghost ship from tracking *The Silent Monsoon.* "So maybe she was telling him the truth."

"I do believe she was," Drassilis replied.

Annette cleared her throat softly. "Far be it for me to suggest something that puts any of this crew in jeopardy, but have we considered the fact that Deliah has a direct line to the ghosts? I'm only suggesting this if she agrees to do it, and I'd monitor her the entire time."

"To what end?" Athos asked.

"She can tell us where they've gone, or where they're going."

Athos shook his head. "But then they'll know where we are, too."

"They already know where we are, Athos," Annette said with a smile. "If they'd wanted to, they could have dealt with us right then and there."

"If they have the capability to do so," Svetlana said. "Still, I think it's a reasonable idea, if you think she'll be safe, Doc."

"Like I said, I'll monitor her, and if it looks like she's in any form of distress, we'll turn the machine back on and cut off the communications."

"Anyone opposed?" Svetlana asked, looking around the bridge.

Jo shook her head immediately. After a moment, Athos shook his as well.

Nodding, Svetlana called down the speaking tube to the engine room. "I'm sending Athos down to monitor the steam reserves. When he gets there, could the two of you come up?"

"Aye, Captain," Indigo replied.

Athos headed below decks as Svetlana looked at Annette and then Jo. "This could be a really bad idea," she said.

"I know," Annette said, "but we don't know how much time we have before Lady de Whittvy does something with the Gem of the Seas."

"Mother is likely to move quickly," Drassilis said.

Svetlana looked at the automaton, one eyebrow arched. "What makes you say that?"

"Mother has long desired to acquire the Gem of the Seas. It was something I was instructed to refrain from discussing previously. However, I believe, based on your descriptions of Mother's behavior, she may no longer be in full control of her faculties." Drassilis paused for a moment, averting his gaze. "And while my own connection to Mother is nothing like Deliah's, I do sometimes have faint impressions from her."

"Before or after she died?" Annette asked. "Sorry, that's rude."

"No need to apologize, Doctor Campbell," Drassilis said. "I should have told you about this connection earlier. Prior to her death, it worked within her home on Bonebriar. Since her demise, it has been primarily while we are airborne. There was a period of time, when I was deactivated, when I had no connection, to the best of my knowledge."

"You're full of surprises, Drassilis," Svetlana said, "but this could be very helpful. Deliah gets her best connections on platform cities. Your connection is better in the air. Is yours impacted by the anti-Aether device too?"

"Yes, Captain Tereshchenko," Drassilis replied.

"Well, I guess it's a good thing we built that, then. But you could have told us earlier."

"I apologize, Captain Tereshchenko. I am only now learning that what Mother meant by the word 'trust' may not mean the same thing it means when others say it. I have grown to trust you and your crew, in the true sense of the word."

Before Svetlana could reply, Indigo and Deliah clambered up the stairs and onto the bridge, both looking at her expectantly.

Svetlana looked at the two teenagers, regretting the question she needed to ask. They were too young to be risking their lives for the good of the world, but here they were. "Deliah, we need to find the ghosts. They have the Gem."

Deliah's face paled to the point where Svetlana wondered if she might need to catch the girl to keep her from hitting her head when she passed out. Instead, Deliah whispered, "She's going to destroy Heliopolis."

"Among other locations, yes," Svetlana said.

"It's her first target," Deliah said. "She hates it."

"She told you this?" Svetlana asked.

Deliah nodded. "She doesn't like some people there. Mayor Bartram. Some other people too."

"If Lady de Whittvy really is Hortence's mother—" Annette began.

"Then she apparently doesn't care that her daughter still lives there," Svetlana said, nearly grabbing the ship's controls to turn their route toward Heliopolis. She caught herself and shook her head. "Or she really can visit Hortence in her dreams, and ... ugh, ghosts are a mess. Okay, Deliah, here's our question, and we want you to think about this. Indy, we want to know what you think too. Are you willing to try to find the ghosts, if we take down the anti-Aether device?"

Deliah nodded vigorously. "I don't want her to destroy Heliopolis. My friends live there."

Svetlana looked to Indigo, who was watching Deliah closely. Then he turned and nodded at Svetlana. "Mine too. The ones that aren't on the ship or in Dougou, at least."

"You're certain, both of you?" Svetlana asked.

Both teenagers nodded.

"Drassilis?"

"I am prepared, Captain Tereshchenko."

"Well, that was easier than I anticipated," Annette said. "Deliah, we're going to go to a platform city, and I'm going to stay with you to make sure you don't get hurt when you communicate with the ghosts. Okay?"

"We can try from here," Deliah suggested.

"Will that work?" Annette asked.

Deliah shrugged. "Worth a shot."

Without a word, Drassilis rolled over to the anti-Aether device they had installed on the bridge and switched it off. The absence of its soothing hum, along with the silence of the cloud generator, made the bridge eerily quiet, especially since they were moving slowly enough that the wind outside wasn't whistling past.

Deliah walked over to Drassilis, slowly, then sat on the floor beside him, looking up at his overly large eyes. She stretched one hand up to meet his, and he took her hand, looking down at her. When their fingers met, they spoke in unison. "Bonebriar."

~

The Silent Monsoon limped along toward Bonebriar, still replenishing its steam reserves and flying at a much lower elevation than normal. Svetlana wanted to fly more quickly, but their stunt with the cloud generator wouldn't allow them to do so. She scanned the skies as they went, looking for any sign that the Air Fleet had managed to catch the same wind as them.

When she did see another ship, it took her a moment to make sense of what she was seeing. It didn't bear the navy and gold balloons of the Air Fleet, but rather a set of shimmering silvery-gray balloons that gleamed in the rays of the setting sun.

She leapt from her seat when she realized whose ship it was. Lar's *Dove* was only one of the Kavisoli ships, but it was the prettiest of the bunch, at least until his new flagship—the one he wanted her to command, if she took the position as admiral of his future fleet—was complete.

Annette looked up from her book. "Captain?"

"We've got a Kavisoli ship inbound," Svetlana muttered. "How do people keep finding us?"

"Maybe because we have a distinctive balloon pattern?" Athos said, sharing a smile with Jo. "Looks like they're coming up to say hello. You want to take over steering so I can run out the speaking tube, or do you have that under control?"

Svetlana clenched her hands into fists. She didn't really want either. She wanted to see who was on Lar's prize ship, of course, but if it was Lar, she didn't want to talk to him over the speaking tube. The conversation they needed to have wasn't the sort of conversation that both their crews needed to be part of.

The *Dove* swung in a lazy, downward arc, maneuvering to come alongside *The Silent Monsoon*. Lar, at the helm, smiled and waved, then leaned back, causing Svetlana to yelp in surprise. Narci was flying the *Dove* alongside him.

Svetlana's thoughts raced. Had Narci gone to Lar after being released from the Air Fleet? Had she been looking for Svetlana, or just any calm port in a storm? And why was Lar letting her fly his ship?

Before her anger burned too hot, she forced herself to take a deep breath. Had she been in Narci's shoes, recently out of a job, she'd probably look to friendly faces as well. And though Svetlana had never flown with Lar at the helm, there was no doubt that an Air Fleet trained pilot would be more skilled than a hobbyist.

The *Dove* piped out a few blasts of a whistle in a particular pattern, and Svetlana turned to Athos.

"They're asking permission to come aboard," Athos said. "We don't have a fancy whistle system like theirs, so I suppose you can answer by running out the gangplank for them."

Svetlana considered. The other option was for her to ask to board the *Dove*, but then she'd be on Lar's ship. Bringing him over to her ship seemed like it would give her a slightly better position from which to argue. All the better if she could clear the bridge and have this conversation in full view of the cloud generator that was the entire reason she was mad at him.

Finally, she nodded. "Annette, can I get some assistance with the gangplank?"

Annette set down her book, trying to keep a grin from her lips, and nodded. "Sure, Captain."

By the time Svetlana and Annette had maneuvered the gangplank into a position to bridge the gap between the two ships, someone else had taken over flying the *Dove*, and Lar and Narci stood on deck, ready to cross.

"Shall I put on tea?" Annette asked.

"Why not?" Svetlana asked, forcing a note of levity into her voice. Out here in the whipping winds, she wasn't sure she wanted to give Lar the comfort of the bridge. Perhaps they'd just talk here. Narci could go below with Annette, and Athos and Jo could stay on the bridge and watch but not hear Lar and Svetlana's conversation.

"Sveta," Lar murmured as he stepped onto *The Silent Monsoon*. "I'm sorry."

Svetlana choked out a laugh. "Good opening. Let's continue in that vein, shall we?"

Lar's brow furrowed as he shot a glance at Annette, who shrugged. Svetlana couldn't read Annette's expression at this angle, but the doctor followed her shrug with, "Narcissa, good to see you. Care for some tea?"

Narci glanced at Lar, then nodded. "Yes, tea sounds wonderful." There was a hint of confusion in her voice, but she followed Annette all the same.

When the two of them were gone, Lar spoke softly. "I worried that something had happened to you when I didn't hear from you after you left. I understand that you're likely angry with me. Our last conversation left some things unsaid."

Svetlana stared at the deck instead of at Lar. Standing this near to him, she realized she had missed him considerably more than she wanted to admit. He was right about the things left unsaid, too. "Was it your idea or Martin's to call the present a bride gift?" she asked, her voice just loud enough to be heard over the wind.

"Oh, sweet Skyfather," Lar said. "Had I but sent a note, my intentions would have been clear from the start. It was a gift of something my engineers had invented, a prototype I thought you would want to be the first to test. Martin misunderstood my intentions in the gift, I assure you."

Svetlana shook her head, now looking up at Lar. "You understand why I was concerned, then?"

"Yes. Absolutely. Why didn't you ask me sooner?"

"Because I was livid, thinking you'd disregarded my thoughts on marriage, and thought you'd just send gifts until I caved," Svetlana said, throwing her hands up. "It was ... I've been under a lot of stress. I'm still under a lot of stress. I didn't need more."

"What can I do to help?" Lar asked, his arms around Svetlana in an instant.

Svetlana felt herself melting into his embrace, and she had to stop herself. "Not that. Not just yet." As she pulled away, she frowned. "Why is Narci here?"

"Ah, long story," Lar said. "Have you time?"

"Depends," Svetlana said. "Can the *Dove* follow us for a bit? We're on low steam reserves at the moment."

Lar chuckled. "So you've enjoyed the gift?"

Svetlana leveled a glare at him but nodded. "We found out what the magic button does, and it's gotten us out of a pinch. But it'd be best if we could pull in the gangplank and have the *Dove* follow us to Bonebriar."

"Bonebriar?" Lar said. "It seems you've got a long story as well, then, Sveta darling."

"You barely know the half of it," Svetlana said.

~

The *Dove* trailed behind *The Silent Monsoon*, occasionally visible through the high windows in the mess, where Svetlana, Lar, Annette, Athos, and Narci sat. Svetlana had filled Narci and Lar in on what she and her crew had been up to since they'd last spoken.

Narci's story was much shorter. "I've been dismissed from the Fleet."

Svetlana's good eye widened. "What excuse did they make up?"

"They really didn't have to," Narci said. "It was just a matter of time before my insubordination outweighed my usefulness to them. So I hopped on a ship bound for Rrusadon to ask after you lot, and Mayor Kavisoli was kind enough to bring me out here personally."

Svetlana shared a small smile with Lar. She knew he would have leapt on any excuse to come and see her, especially since their last meeting had been fraught with misunderstanding. Now that everything was cleared up, she was glad to have him around. "What's next, then?" she asked Narci.

"For now, if you'll have me, I'd like to sign on to the *Monsoon*." Narci looked at Lar, but Svetlana didn't turn to see Lar's expression quickly enough. She suspected the two had shared some silent communication, though.

"We'd be happy to have you," Svetlana said. "If it's temporary, we'll have to work out your share—"

Narci waved her hand. "I'm happy to take a half-share for now. I'm not ready to make any commitments yet."

"And what about you?" Svetlana asked, turning her attention to Lar.

"Alas, I can't stay long. I have a city to run, after all, once I get done with this idle pleasure cruise."

"Likely excuse," Svetlana said, grinning widely at him. "Once you've cleared things up with Martin, would you send him to Bonebriar? We may be in need of backup in the near future."

Before Lar could respond, a double thump came through the speaking tube from the bridge. "That'll be Jo," Svetlana said, scrambling from her chair and rushing above deck. Several other sets of footfalls followed her.

Jo nodded at the captain when she arrived, then pressed her lips into a firm line and inclined her head to the starboard, where the *Dove* hovered. Just beyond that ship, another ship loomed in the distance, this one recognizable with its navy and gold balloons and flag.

"No rest for the wicked," Svetlana murmured. She turned back to see who had followed her up from the mess.

Lar was in the lead. "If you want to get back to Rrusadon, you'd best signal your ship to retrieve you now," she said, planting a quick kiss on his lips. "I'll be back soon, I hope."

"Likewise," he said, returning her kiss with one that lingered. "Martin's on the *Dove*. If you can wait a moment after I'm returned, I'll send him to you. With an apology waiting on his lips."

Svetlana smiled and nodded. "Please do. We can use his help."

Lar turned to Narci. "Consider my offer?"

Narci nodded, and Lar hurried onto the deck, waving his arms to signal the *Dove*.

"His offer?" Svetlana asked. "Should I be jealous?"

"Unlikely. I'll tell you the details later," Narci said, squinting in the direction of the ship. "Mid-sized. Half a dozen cannon, at best."

"How are the steam reserves?" Athos asked, looking at the gauges beside Jo. "Damn, only 75 percent."

"That might be enough," Svetlana said. "We're near Bonebriar, right?"

Jo nodded as she glanced up at the clock. "Ten minutes."

"Air Fleet can catch this ship far faster than that," Narci said, scoffing at Jo's estimate.

"Help her with the helm," Svetlana said, nodding toward the open steering column. She opened the speaking tube to the engine room. "Indy, how much more speed can you give us?"

"Little bit," he replied. "Once the other ship isn't pacing us."

The crew on the bridge of *The Silent Monsoon* watched as the *Dove* moved alongside their ship and Lar made the crossing. In short order, Martin hurried from the bridge and crossed to *The Silent Monsoon*, still struggling into a coat and holding a hunk of bread in his teeth. Once he was onboard, Svetlana waved once more to Lar, and then turned to Jo and Narci.

"Let's move."

CHAPTER FIFTEEN

The tree-filled canopy of Bonebriar rose ahead, and the Air Fleet ship loomed behind *The Silent Monsoon*. Svetlana had insisted her crew remain in enclosed portions of the ship during this approach, to avoid any potential run-ins with the arboreal kraken that lived in Bonebriar's trees. Athos, in particular, had been pleased with that decision.

Even now, a few tentacles poked tentatively from the canopy, as though they were "tasting" the air above the island.

"Skirt the side?" Svetlana asked Jo.

Jo shook her head. "Use the kraken."

Frowning, Svetlana asked, "Don't you think we ought to avoid it?"

Jo nodded. "But they shouldn't," she said, tossing her head back, toward the pursuing Air Fleet ship.

"Could you explain this arboreal kraken to me?" Narci asked.

"Of course," Drassilis began. "The arboreal kraken—"

"No," Svetlana said, cutting him off. "Trust me, Narci. If you've eaten in the last day, you don't want Drassilis's explanation."

"Okay, but," Narci said, "what in the abyss is an arboreal kraken?"

As if in answer to her question, more tentacles emerged from the tree canopy, stretching and grasping their way toward *The Silent Monsoon*. Jo maneuvered the ship away from them, but they continued to probe the air, searching.

"Captain, did you see—?" Martin began.

"What was that?" Narci asked, cutting Martin's words short, her voice flat but with an edge of fear tinging it.

"Kraken that lives in the trees," Svetlana said. "Alright, Jo, how are we baiting the trap?"

Jo's gaze went directly to the cloud generator. "Fast drop."

Svetlana frowned. "What, like directly above the kraken? That's a horrible plan."

"Fly past, then drop," Athos said. "Yeah?"

Jo nodded, huffing out a breath of frustration. She nodded at Martin, then jerked her head toward the cloud generator.

Martin seemed to understand her pantomime and went to stand beside the device. He turned it on, but fiddled with a couple of knobs, and though the device whined like it had been started, no cloud appeared around the ship.

Jo nodded again. "My mark." Then she looked at Svetlana. "Stay even."

"You want me to lock the controls to keep us even?" Svetlana asked.

Jo shook her head. "No, just in case."

Svetlana nodded, and Jo swung the directional wheel to bring *The Silent Monsoon* toward the arboreal kraken and the dense tree cover. They were flying significantly above the tops of the trees, but the arboreal kraken's tentacles had a lot more reach than Svetlana was comfortable with. She trusted Jo with her ship, and with the lives of herself and her crew, but even so, a cold sweat broke out across the back of her neck. She almost turned to make sure the Air Fleet ship still followed them, but based on Narci's tight expression, the other ship was clearly still in pursuit, and possibly gaining.

Jo's gaze darted around the canopy as she steered, homing in on tentacles as they emerged and disappeared. It reminded Svetlana of watching small birds dart in and out of crevices on the undersides of platform cities. Few could track all the birds at once, but Jo seemed to be doing a fine job of remaining aware of the majority of the arboreal kraken's tentacles.

A boom sounded behind *The Silent Monsoon*, and Narci inhaled sharply. "Do you have cannon on this ship?"

"One," Svetlana said.

"And no cannoneers," Narci said, shaking her head.

"Hey, I cannoneered for a while," Athos said.

Jo's sharp hiss quieted him.

"No hit," Indigo's voice echoed up from the engine room.

Narci let out a sigh of relief. "If it's all the same, can Athos and I man the cannon?"

Svetlana nodded. "There's not much shot to be had, so only use it if you're sure of a hit. And if a tentacle heads your way ... well, that'd be a good use of a shot."

Narci nodded and hurried below deck. Athos paused only long enough to kiss Jo's forehead and then followed Narci.

Svetlana glanced at Jo, who was still scanning the treetops. A few tentacles still darted up occasionally, but they seemed to have lessened now. "Drassilis, how many tentacles—"

"Drop," Jo said, louder than she'd spoken since they'd rescued her, before Svetlana could finish her question.

Martin punched the button on the side of the cloud generator, and *The Silent Monsoon* plummeted below the treeline, greens and browns replacing the blues and whites of the skies.

Svetlana tried to ignore the multitude of branches battering the hull of her ship and the balloons, at the same time she was trying to ignore the yelps emanating from below decks. "Guess we should've given them more warning," she murmured.

Jo shrugged and glanced through the back window of the bridge.

For the first time, the crew saw the bulk of the arboreal kraken, a bloated green and grey mass, as it floated between the trees and emerged from the canopy. The motion was followed by a crunching sound, but *The Silent Monsoon* didn't waver.

Then Jo nodded at Svetlana. "Up."

Svetlana pulled back on the altitude controls to return her ship to the space above the canopy. She spared only the quickest of glances at the Air Fleet ship, now entangled within the grasp of the arboreal kraken. Their cannon would allow them to chase the beast off, more likely than not, but at least Jo's maneuvering had gotten *The Silent Monsoon* the bit of breathing room it so desperately needed right now.

~

The ghost ship was docked when they reached the aboveground residential portion of Bonebriar. Narci sighed as she looked at it. "I really wish you had more cannon, Sveta."

"Me too," Svetlana admitted. "Jo, let's dock as far from them as we can, just for our own safety."

Jo nodded and swung the ship into position to dock at the opposite end of the docking area.

Svetlana continued to man the altitude controls as they landed, but her gaze, along with those of everyone else on the bridge, remained locked on the ghost ship. A handful of ghosts watched *The Silent Monsoon* from onboard their ship, creating a palpable tension even across the space between the ships.

"So, what's the plan, Captain?" Athos asked when the ship had come to a full rest on the docking struts.

"Find the Gem. Take it," Svetlana said tersely.

"Any thoughts on where to start looking?" Annette asked, gaze still fixed on the ghost ship.

Svetlana considered the options. The ghost ship had a larger crew, and a good portion of them were watching *The Silent Monsoon* even now. Trying to sneak onto their ship would be impossible, and she couldn't even be sure the Gem would be onboard. Looking there last seemed reasonable. "I'm going to Lady de Whittvy's house," she said, but then hesitated. Going alone was dangerous. If Lady de Whittvy was at her house, that might be a level of complications for which none of them were prepared. She also wanted most of the crew onboard the ship in case they needed to make a quick escape. "Athos, fancy coming with?"

"Blades, you said?" he asked.

"I'll take that as a yes."

"Would you like a third?" Martin asked, fingering the hilt of one of the knives he wore on his belt.

"I appreciate your enthusiasm, Martin, but this isn't a job for a large group," Svetlana said. "Stay here and keep an eye on the ghost ship. Do you know communications signals?"

Martin shrugged. "Well enough."

"We don't have the fancy whistles that the *Dove* has, but you can get Annette to show you what we do have. If anything requires our attention, sound the alarm, and we'll get back as quickly as we can."

Svetlana and Athos left *The Silent Monsoon*, still watching the ghost ship. None of the ghostly crew followed them, at least not as far as they could see. It didn't matter much to Svetlana if they were being followed, and with a crew that could slip in and out of

Aetherwhere at will, it seemed better to assume their movements, especially here, would be tracked.

The front of Lady de Whittvy's house had not been rebuilt since the Air Fleet had destroyed it, giving Svetlana and Athos a mostly clear view into the front rooms of the house. Piles of rubble still obscured portions of the space. Lady de Whittvy's tell-tale ginger hair, even muted as it was after death, was not visible.

"We'll take the back way up to her lab." Svetlana paused, recalling that Lady de Whittvy had done something that looked a bit like overloading all of the devices she had within her lab before their departure. It had likely destroyed her work there, if not the room in its entirety. "Or whatever's left of it."

Athos nodded and followed Svetlana around the side of the house, his hand on the hilt of his sword. There wouldn't be enough room to draw it in the narrow space between the buildings, but Svetlana understood the comfort of having a weapon close at hand, her own hand resting on the hilt of a knife tucked into her belt. If the ghosts were following them, this would make a perfect pinch point, where they would be trapped and barely able to defend themselves.

Svetlana breathed a sigh of relief when they reached Lady de Whittvy's backyard. The back door stood ajar, and as they got closer, they could see it had been knocked askew from its hinges. Inside the house, most of the space looked as though it had been ransacked.

"I thought they all called her Mother around here, and worshipped her like a goddess," Athos said.

"I think this was Air Fleet," Svetlana said, nodding at the boot prints marring the stone dust on the floor. "Probably digging around after she was dead." She gestured to the side with her head. "Back ways are over here."

The door leading to the secret stairway was open, and Svetlana hesitated just outside of it, listening for any movement above. There seemed to be a faint buzzing, but she couldn't tell for certain if it was there or just what her mind was filling the silence with.

"You hear anything?" she whispered.

Athos shook his head. "Maybe my heartbeat."

Svetlana chuckled softly, drew her knife, and led the way up the stairs. Behind her, Athos unsheathed his blade just loudly enough for her to hear that he'd done so.

As they neared the lab, there wasn't an electrical buzzing sound like Svetlana thought she had heard, but there was noise coming from the room. Pausing outside the door, Svetlana peeked around the jamb.

Inside the ruined lab, with equipment strewn about and half dismantled, Lady de Whittvy stood with her back to the door. In front of her was a table, with several books open and rapidly flipping through their pages, causing the slight murmur of sound that had carried from the room.

Svetlana tiptoed through the doorway, but her attempt at silence was for naught.

Lady de Whittvy spun to face her immediately, not even a wisp of surprise in her expression. The books paused in their flipping, some of the pages suspended as though they'd been frozen in time. "You just don't stop, do you?"

"She really doesn't," Athos said drily, moving to stand to Svetlana's left, his body thrumming with a readiness to strike.

"Just checking up on you," Svetlana said with a stiff grin. "Air Fleet is inbound."

"Ah, to be expected, I suppose," Lady de Whittvy said. "Would you like to help me dispatch them, then?"

"We've slowed them down, but they won't stop, even if we stop this ship. You need to negotiate with the High Council if you're going to stop the Fleet from coming after you for the rest of your days."

"At least until I drop a platform city or two," Lady de Whittvy said.

Svetlana shook her head. "You said you'd negotiate first."

"Call it aggressive negotiations," Lady de Whittvy spat back. "Svetlana, the High Council won't acquiesce any other way."

"This is not what we agreed to," Svetlana said, clenching her left fist. She struggled to keep herself from raising her knife in her right hand, not wanting to threaten Lady de Whittvy directly.

"The only way you're going to keep your precious platform cities in the air is if you take the Gem from me and destroy it," Lady de Whittvy said.

Svetlana chided herself mentally. She should have known better than to trust Lady de Whittvy when she realized the noblewoman was working with the ghosts. She'd let herself be swayed by false promises. Lady de Whittvy was right. Destruction of the Gem should ensure no one ever used it for nefarious purposes. What else it might do remained to be seen.

"Fine, have it your way," Svetlana said, stepping toward Lady de Whittvy. "Where's the Gem?"

"Not here," Lady de Whittvy scoffed. She looked to her left and inclined her head in Svetlana's direction, her gaze unfocused.

A crowd of half a dozen ghosts swarmed around Lady de Whittvy, then surged toward Svetlana and Athos, trailing more ghosts in their wake.

Svetlana backpedaled, pulling Athos along with her. Her heel struck some of the rubble on the floor of Lady de Whittvy's lab, halting her backward motion. She swung her knife at the nearest ghost, who parried the attack with his own blade. No ring of metal on metal accompanied the action, but her swing was cut short all the same.

Forcing her blade forward, Svetlana tried to turn her opponent's weapon to the side. The ghost held his ground, his strength at least equal to hers.

Meanwhile, Athos had leapt forward and engaged two of the ghosts. He had driven them both back a few steps, but now other ghosts flanked him.

"We've got to get out of here," Svetlana said, sweeping one foot behind her to find a way around the rubble while she still fought the ghost in front of her. She ducked a blow from that ghost and picked up a piece of metal from the floor, which she then threw at one of the ghosts flanking Athos. The left-handed throw wasn't particularly accurate, but it at least pulled the ghost's attention to her instead of Athos.

"Follow your girlfriend?" Athos asked, gesturing toward Lady de Whittvy, who had slipped out a door Svetlana hadn't noticed before.

"She's. Not. My. Girlfriend," Svetlana insisted, her words punctuated with grunts as she kicked at the ghost to her left while parrying blows from the ghost to her right. She drove back the latter an extra step and moved to skirt around him. "But yes, follow her."

Athos disengaged from his opponents and backed up against Svetlana, covering their retreat as she charged toward the door where Lady de Whittvy had gone.

Into a closet. And the noblewoman was nowhere to be seen.

"Well," Athos said. "Back out into the fray?"

Svetlana nodded. "Gonna be a bit more difficult now."

The ghosts had regrouped and now blocked Svetlana and Athos's way out of the closet where Lady de Whittvy had led them. While looking for any opening, Svetlana also tapped her foot against the closet wall behind them.

"What are you doing?" Athos asked.

"Hoping for a secret door. No luck. Let's do this." Svetlana pushed off from the wall and charged forward.

Svetlana and Athos remained side by side now, nearly touching, making them a larger target, but one that could defend itself on either side. One of the ghosts swung at Athos, and Svetlana deflected the blow, and then Athos returned the favor by stopping the sword that slashed toward her open side. They moved slowly from the closet to the next door, the one Svetlana knew would lead into the house proper.

For their part, the ghosts were relentless. Any attempt at an attack by either Svetlana or Athos was met with at least two attacks from the ghosts. Nor were the ghosts only reacting to attacks; those not directly in Svetlana and Athos's path harried them from the sides, while the captain and her first mate split their attention between movement and defense, punctuated by their increasingly rare opportunities to attack.

As they neared the doorway, Athos shifted his position to parry an attack at their rear, as a ghost slid through the wall behind them. "How are they doing this?" he growled.

"Aetherwhere," Svetlana replied. "Faerie Queen be blessed and all that rubbish."

"I'm glad she's not your girlfriend, Sveta," Athos said. "I don't think I could handle knowing you're in love with a ghost."

"Thanks, I think."

Several of the ghosts pressed forward, driving Svetlana and Athos back several paces, and blocking their passageway to the door out of the map room.

"This isn't going well. Two steps forward, three steps back, and all that." He glanced over his shoulder. "Maybe we can make a hole in the wall of that closet."

Before Svetlana responded, another figure appeared in the doorway to the room, drawing the ghosts' attention. Hortence Bartram, the daughter of Heliopolis's mayor and, allegedly, Lady de

Whittvy, scanned the room, a smile dancing across her lips when she spotted Svetlana.

"Captain! I thought I saw your ship on our approach."

"What are you doing here?" Svetlana asked.

Hortence looked around. "Getting you out of here, first, I think." She lunged forward with her delicate rapier and began clearing a path through the ghosts.

Svetlana seized the opportunity and pulled Athos behind her toward the doorway. With the added distraction of a third combatant on their side, the ghosts were easily removed from their path, and Svetlana and Athos made their way into the hallway outside of the map room.

Once Svetlana and Athos had slipped through the doorway, the attacks from the ghosts stopped, as though they could not pass this threshold into the real world.

"Oh, now here's a twist," Athos said, grinning back at the ghosts. "You lot can't follow us, eh?"

"We have eyes everywhere, pretty boy," one of the ghosts replied, this one a buxom woman who appeared to be sincere in her attraction to Athos.

"Sorry, my dear. I'm taken." Athos blew her a kiss. "Another time, perhaps?"

Hortence cleared her throat. "This is all fine and well, but where is my mother?"

Svetlana smiled. "Good to see you, Miss Bartram. She's probably headed for the ghost ship. Let's go."

CHAPTER SIXTEEN

The ghost ship had taken off by the time Svetlana, Athos, and Hortence returned to *The Silent Monsoon*. Looming in the distance in the opposite direction was the Air Fleet ship, clearly headed toward the ghost ship.

"Perfect," Athos said. "We can let the Air Fleet deal with the ghosts."

"No, we can't," Hortence said. "They're going to be looking for me."

Svetlana arched her eyebrow as she looked at Hortence. "Oh? Why's that?"

"Well, it's a bit of story." Hortence shrugged. "The short version is that they're with me, sort of?"

Svetlana glanced between the mayor's daughter, the approaching Air Fleet ship, and the departing ghost ship. "The Gem must be on the ghost ship. We don't want the Air Fleet getting hold of it, so we need to get the Air Fleet out of here and catch up to the ghosts. You can tell us the rest of the story on the way. Athos, head below. I'll send Narci down to help you with the cannon."

Athos shook his head. "We're not going to hold off an Air Fleet ship with our cannon. Unless you want me to start loading it with Jo's costume jewelry and hope they get distracted by the shiny things."

"We'll figure something out." Svetlana paused, considering her options for how to distribute her now larger crew. "Wait, Athos, I need you on the bridge for comms. You can read Jo, signal with Indy, and talk to Narci and Annette. We need to be able to move fast and with precision. Miss Bartram, you can stay on the bridge and explain what's happening."

Athos and Hortence both nodded and followed Svetlana onto the bridge.

Svetlana opened the speaking tube to the engine room before she started her quick summary. "The ghosts have the Gem, Air Fleet's incoming, and we've got Miss Hortence Bartram joining us onboard. Narci and Martin, you're on the cannon. Do what you can to threaten the Air Fleet and get them to break off pursuit. Athos is on comms. Indy, he'll be signaling you and Deliah in the engine room, so listen for that and tell Deliah what needs to be done. Drassilis, go below and help with the engines. Annette, stand by to help with the cannon if they call for you. Jo?" Svetlana smiled. "We're going to need to board the ghost ship."

Jo raised her eyebrows and pointed to herself.

"No, not you," Svetlana said as Narci and Annette left the bridge. "I'll take Athos, Narci, Martin, and Miss Bartram, I think. We're going to want you to keep the *Monsoon* below the ghost ship, just in case they decide to jump into Aetherwhere and strand us in the middle of the sky."

Jo nodded and moved to the steering column, freeing up the altitude controls for Svetlana. The ship pulled out of its berth smoothly and raised to an elevation where it could interpose itself between the ghost ship and the Air Fleet ship.

"Sandbar and a coral reef," Athos muttered, swiveling his head to keep an eye on both the ship they were pursuing and their pursuers. "Well, Air Fleet's backing off."

"Cannon must be showing," Svetlana said.

The Silent Monsoon flew through the skies, gaining on the ghost ship. Adjusting the controls until the two ships flew at the same altitude, Svetlana then locked the altitude controls. The Air Fleet ship had fallen farther behind, though their reasoning for doing so was not apparent.

"So, story?" Svetlana asked Hortence.

"Right. Time being short, I'll explain this as quickly as I can. Having not heard from you for some time, I began making my own arrangements for a ship to retrieve my mother's Cranglimmering. I was able to hire a ship on the promise of a share of the profits from the sale of the whiskey, but word got back to the Swaisbrooks—" Hortence grimaced at the mention of her potential fiancé's name. The son of a High Councilor, he was an appropriate match for the daughter of a mayor, but Hortence had previously indicated her disinterest in a political marriage, or any other sort of marriage. "—and they insisted I needed a full Air Fleet escort. No doubt because they hope to get their hands on the Cranglimmering, one way or another."

"So where is your ship?" Svetlana asked.

"If all is well, docked in an out of the way location at Bonebriar, awaiting me finding the Cranglimmering, so they can then determine the best way to load it onto their ship. I had thought we'd lost the Air Fleet entirely, but perhaps they just found a more interesting ship to follow."

"One or the other, I suppose they did," Svetlana murmured. "There's a good likelihood your mother is on the ghost ship presently. She has something we need, which is why we're boarding them. Are you prepared—"

"Let me at her," Hortence said, not even letting Svetlana ask her the question. "I've come for her whiskey, but I'll help you stop her, too."

"Do you know what she's been planning?"

"I know she came to me in a dream and told me to leave Heliopolis."

Svetlana arched an eyebrow, surprised Lady de Whittvy had made such a gesture. "When did that happen?"

"Some weeks ago." Hortence shrugged. "It took me some time to make the arrangements for the ship."

"Ah," Svetlana said, gazing past Hortence as though the sky had suddenly become the most interesting thing in the world.

Hortence crossed her arms over her chest. "There's something you're not telling me."

"We haven't the time to go into all the details now, but if your mother has her way, there won't be a Heliopolis left to return to," Svetlana said, still not meeting Hortence's gaze.

"I see," Hortence said, her voice steely. "Then as I said, let me at her. We'll sort out the rest later."

Svetlana nodded. "I'm glad to have you with us, then. Athos, can you set up a signal—something with light—so Jo can let us know if the Air Fleet is threatening the *Monsoon*? I'd like to have a ship to come home to once we find the Gem."

"Better than that," Athos said. "Steam signals. From what I've seen of the ghost ship, clouds pass through it, rather than it passing through clouds, like we do. I think I can tweak this cloud generator so it'll send a puff up."

"How long will that take?" Svetlana asked.

"Faster with some help." Athos tapped a pattern on the floor with his heel and toe of one foot. Svetlana didn't know all the details of the code Athos and Indy had worked out, but a moment later, Martin emerged from below.

The Silent Monsoon moved nearly side by side with the ghost ship, not quite ready for boarding, and Svetlana began to pace as Athos quickly explained to Martin what they needed to do. He nodded and turned a few knobs on the device that created clouds from excess steam.

"Shall we give it a test?" Athos asked.

Svetlana nodded and watched out the windows of the bridge as Martin tapped a button. Plumes of steam spouted from two places Svetlana could see, and she heard the hiss of escaping steam behind her as well.

"Well done," Svetlana said with a chuckle, stalking over to the speaking tube. "Narci, come up. You're invited to the boarding party."

~

Svetlana, Athos, Martin, and Hortence had no difficulty crossing the gangplank they'd run from their ship to the aft portion of the ghost ship's deck. Narci, on the other hand, still stood on board *The Silent Monsoon*.

"Is this ... safe?" she asked, her dark skin going ashen, popping her freckles out in sharp relief.

"Just don't look down," Svetlana said. "It's like any other ship to ship boarding.

Narci shook her head. "I mean the ghost ship. It can disappear into Aetherwhere whenever it wants, right? So what's stopping them from realizing they're being boarded and just vanishing?"

"If we board quickly and spread out, we lessen the chances they figure that out, Narci," Athos said. He held out his hand. "C'mon."

Narci gave him a tight nod and hurried across the gangplank, gaze locked with Svetlana as she did. As soon as she was on the ghost ship, Svetlana and Athos pushed their gangplank back onto the *Monsoon*. The ship then dropped in altitude and maneuvered out of sight, below the ghost ship.

Narci stared at her feet on the mostly solid-looking deck, still looking pale and worried. She took a tentative step forward, visibly relieved when her foot didn't sink through the deck.

Svetlana snapped to draw Narci's attention. "Okay, seriously. It's like any boat of the Fleet. Yes, things can change in a hurry, but it's not like you ran around every ship you were posted to expecting to be pitched off into the sky at any moment. Besides which, Jo is going to be ready to catch us if we fall."

Narci nodded, setting her lips in a firm line. She still looked nervous, but at least some determination now shone in her eyes. That was going to have to be good enough for this excursion.

Muffled voices came from around the corner, drawing everyone's attention. A pair of ghosts, walking on the deck just like Svetlana's crew, stepped into view and noticed the cluster of still-living invaders.

Athos drew his sword and advanced on the ghosts, twirling the blade in his hand casually. The ghosts fumbled for their own weapons as Narci followed Athos, drawing her rapier. Martin hung back near Svetlana and Hortence, but unsheathed one of his lighter knives, well-balanced for throwing.

"You three stick together," Svetlana said. "Hortence and I are going below."

Athos nodded just before he engaged the first of the ghosts, and Svetlana and Hortence slipped away from the grunting that accompanied swordplay between the ghosts and her crew.

The below deck halls of the ghost ship were quiet. It seemed the ghosts who had encountered them hadn't raised an alarm, which was a good start. Svetlana kept her knife at the ready and slunk down the hallway, back pressed to the wall. She paused to listen at the first doorway they encountered, but everything remained silent as they moved.

Leading with her blind eye wasn't ideal, but she'd chosen the wrong side of the hall to slink down if she wanted to be armed and ahead of Hortence. Svetlana leaned forward just enough to get a glimpse into the room beyond the doorway. No one lurked within, so she took a step inside to get a better look at the room's contents. It looked as if it had once been the ship's mess, but all that remained was the ghostly image of a scarred table and the small amount of counter and cabinet space a ship could afford to have. Even the doors to the cabinet had a wavering translucent quality to them, enough so Svetlana was certain they didn't contain the Gem.

She looked at Hortence. "I don't suppose you have any thoughts on how to find the Gem?"

"Gem?" Hortence asked. "What gem?"

"Right, I guess I left that part out. Your mother has the Gem of the Seas, or did quite recently. We have reason to believe it's somewhere on this ship."

Hortence arched an eyebrow. "The Gem of the Seas? Isn't that just a myth?"

"No, it's real, and as best as we can tell, it does what the legends say. If the oceans stop boiling, the platform cities drop."

"That explains what you meant about no Heliopolis to return to." Hortence laughed softly. "And here I thought you anticipated her bombing it. At any rate, I suppose we should start with my mother, don't you?"

Svetlana nodded. "I wish we didn't have to hunt her down, though. Couldn't she come to face us? Or leave the Gem somewhere convenient where we can just snatch it up and be on our way."

"No one's that lucky, Captain," Hortence said.

Svetlana grimaced. "Right. Let's keep looking."

The next room Svetlana poked her head into was occupied. She jerked her head back quickly, a frown creasing her brow. She recognized the room's inhabitant. She'd seen him before, when they had boarded the ghost ship looking for Lady de Whittvy, shortly after the scientist had been kidnapped. He wore a hairstyle that had gone out of fashion several hundred years ago, and his clothing matched that era.

She couldn't be certain without risking another look, but she also thought he was wearing the Gem of the Seas atop his head.

Leaning back toward Hortence, she said, "The Gem's here, your mother's not. But there is another ghost, and he likely won't give it up without a fight. Go find Athos and Narci and Martin. I'm going to need all of your help."

Hortence nodded and headed back the way they'd come from, instead of forward to the nearer set of stairs that would require her to pass in front of the open doorway.

For her part, Svetlana waited outside the room. The ghost wearing the Gem didn't look as though he was much of a fighter, but having the others to help her pin him down and prevent him from escaping their clutches would be beneficial. She'd seen too many ghosts ignore the restrictions of walls and floors, and she somehow doubted possessing the Gem of the Seas would slow this ghost down.

From within the room came a faint whistling that resolved itself into a tune. At first, she couldn't quite place it, but when the song reached the chorus, Svetlana recognized it as an old sailing shanty still popular among those in the shipping business, though they'd changed the word "seas" to "skies" in the intervening years. The song had a long history, dating back all the way to the time before the Republic.

And that was when Svetlana realized it wasn't just any old ghost wearing the Gem of the Seas—it was the ghost of the first High General, Lord Eleazer Throckmorton. She'd passed under his portrait countless times at the Air Fleet Headquarters, and now she couldn't believe she hadn't identified him more quickly the first time she saw him.

She itched to walk into the room and confront him, but the rest of her crew hadn't made their appearance yet. She resisted the urge to tip their hand too early.

Footsteps made their way toward where Svetlana waited. She scanned the hallway in both directions but saw no one. With the sudden realization that the ghost of High General Throckmorton was on the move, Svetlana whirled and stepped into the doorway, bringing herself nearly nose to nose with the ghost.

Throckmorton cocked his head to the side, eyes narrowing. "Can I help you?"

Svetlana raised her knife slightly. "You could go back and sit at that fine desk of yours for starters."

He eyed the knife and raised his hands in front of him, then took a handful of steps backward. "Will this do?"

Svetlana scanned the room, verifying that no other ghosts appeared to be present, and there were no visible weapons he might access. "Far be it from me to issue orders to someone of such renown, but I would like to have that crown of yours."

Gesturing toward the Gem of the Seas, Throckmorton smiled faintly. "Yes, of course. You're the one Lady Elinor told me wants to destroy it."

Svetlana nodded. "That's right. I take it you'd rather keep it intact?"

"I have no strong feelings on the subject, to be perfectly honest," Throckmorton replied. "Neither option will bring me back from the dead nor restore the glory of the empire."

"What would the options do, then?"

"If the Gem remains intact, it gives the bearer the ability to control the seas, as promised. If it is destroyed, then the seas continued to boil, as they did millennia ago, before our forefathers crafted the Gem."

"The oceans boiled before?"

Throckmorton nodded. "Our forefathers, if you look back far enough, scrabbled what little they could from rocks in the midst of a boiling sea. Then they created this Gem to control the oceans. When it was lost, the seas boiled once again."

Svetlana chuckled softly. Apparently being long dead gave one much more insight into the minds of men than she had previously suspected. "So if you've got the Gem, why haven't you returned things to the way they once were?"

Now it was Throckmorton's turn to chuckle. "It seems it must be wielded by one of the living in order to have its effect on the waters."

"I see," Svetlana said. "I assume Lady Elinor has a plan for that?"

"Well, I didn't before, but you might just have presented me with one, Sveta darling," Lady de Whittvy said as she slid through the wall to stand near High General Throckmorton.

CHAPTER SEVENTEEN

Svetlana took a step back from the two ghosts now in front of her but hesitated before she took a second. Raucous sounds approached in the hallway, a mix of running footfalls, grunts, and screams. One of the latter sounds was identifiable as Athos, fortunately grunting and not screaming.

Hortence rushed into the room ahead of the combat and froze in the doorway, looking between Lady de Whittvy, Svetlana, and High General Throckmorton, with wide eyes. She didn't speak, but her eyes narrowed, and she raised her sword.

A knife flew down the hallway, and a moment after, Martin slipped past Hortence. "Don't block the way, Miss Bartram. Plenty of ghosts for all of us to send on to their second demise." He took stock of the room and chuckled as he readied a throwing knife. "Plenty."

Narci slid into the room with a ghost hot on her heels. She fended off one attack, and Svetlana jumped into the fray to block a second attack that would have caught Narci's side. "Gem?" Narci breathed when she saw Svetlana.

"Not quite," Svetlana replied, pointing toward the High General.

Athos's sword plunged through the ghost Narci and Svetlana were facing, and he smiled at them over the shoulder of the rapidly disappearing ghost. His expression fell quickly as he took in the rest of the room, but then he whirled away to deal with other ghosts in the hallway.

"Enough," Lady de Whittvy said, but the sounds of fighting did not abate. She held out her hand to Hortence and smiled. "Hortence, my darling daughter?"

"No," Svetlana said, grabbing Hortence by the shoulder.

Hortence shuddered under Svetlana's grip, somehow transfixed by her mother's gaze, but she didn't move closer to Lady de Whittvy.

"You're not going to win, Svetlana," Lady de Whittvy said softly. "If not my daughter, I'll find another living person who can wield the Gem." Her gaze flickered to Narci. "Maybe your friend here, maybe your friend back on Rrusadon. So many options."

"What happened to not using the Gem until you'd spoken to the High Council?" Svetlana asked.

Lady de Whittvy shrugged. "You and I both know they won't change their ways over something they don't even believe in. Perhaps I'll still start small, if you give me what I want. Leave Rrusadon for later?"

"No," Hortence murmured, softly at first, but her voice rose in intensity. "No, no. You'd kill Father!"

Lady de Whittvy shrugged. "Darling, you know he only wants to marry you off to increase his own standing. He's never had another thought in the world other than being important."

"I can take care of myself," Hortence said, advancing toward Lady de Whittvy with the narrow point of her sword leveled toward her mother's neck. "Give my friends the Gem."

"Well, that's rather decisive, don't you think?" Athos said from the doorway. The sounds of fighting had died down, but there were still footfalls in the distance.

Throckmorton shook his head. "Lady Elinor is right, you know. The High Council can't be reasoned with. And there are plenty of people who want to see them fall. Yourself included, if I understand correctly."

"I want to see them fall, yes," Svetlana said, "but I don't want thousands of people to have to die in the process."

"Clearly, you've never fought a war," Throckmorton replied.

"I have, but that was in the past. I don't intend to engage in another if I don't have to," Svetlana spat back. "We can end this one now, before you begin it."

In response, Throckmorton pulled a rapier from thin air.

"I think we'll take that as a no," Narci muttered.

Svetlana stepped toward High General Throckmorton, holding out her left hand, her knife in her right hand still at the ready. "Give me the Gem, and no one gets hurt."

Throckmorton slashed his blade through the air, aiming for Svetlana's open hand.

She pulled back quickly, maintaining her fighting stance. Narci and Hortence moved to her left side and Athos and Martin flanked her on the right, though she only felt their presence rather than seeing it.

Svetlana would have liked the odds of all of them making it out of here safely had armed ghosts not begun streaming through the walls.

Several of the ghosts immediately moved into position to guard both Throckmorton and Lady de Whittvy, creating a partially transparent wall between Svetlana and her crew and their quarries.

Though Lady de Whittvy and this swarm of ghosts had come through the walls to enter the High General's office, none of them seemed to be exiting that way. Throckmorton moved behind his desk, putting more distance between himself and his attackers.

"He can't get out," Svetlana said, just loudly enough for Athos, Narci, Martin, and Hortence to hear her. "Get these guys off him, and I'll pin him down."

With Athos and Martin to her right, Svetlana couldn't see their reactions, but Narci and Hortence both nodded sharply and waded into the fray with the ghosts. The odds were overwhelming, but the majority of the ghosts proved to be easy opponents. The two women dispatched several of them with little difficulty.

Svetlana looked for an opening to get past the ghosts, working alongside the others to create such an opportunity. As she negotiated her position, she caught occasional glimpses of Athos and Martin attempting to get past the ghosts as well.

When she returned her attention in front of her, she spotted an opening in the line and moved toward it. Two blurs of motion slowed her—first, a wispy ginger-topped figure inside of the line, and second, dark hair and solid clothing that could not possibly be a ghost.

Svetlana collided with Narci, and Narci gasped. It took a moment for Svetlana to realize her former lover's outcry was not from their collision, but rather from the ghostly sword now retreating from her side, leaving a trail of blood in its wake.

Lady de Whittvy chuckled softly, gaze locked on Narci. "Well, I suppose we're even now." She moved away from the gap as Narci collapsed to her knees.

Svetlana knelt beside Narci, hands frantically flapping near the wound, which had already colored Narci's shirt crimson.

"Get the Gem," Narci muttered through clenched teeth.

Svetlana glanced up. No ghosts had filled the opening in the line, and High General Throckmorton now cowered in the corner. She peeled off her vest and pressed it to Narci's side. "Hold that tight," she said before she plunged through the gap toward Throckmorton.

Svetlana checked for Lady de Whittvy's location, but the noblewoman and her daughter had both vanished. She kept her knife at the ready as she crouched near the floor and worked her way to the High General.

He had already removed the crown when she reached him and held it out with a shaking hand. "Take it," he wailed. "Just leave me be."

Svetlana snatched the crown from his hand. "Call off your men."

"They won't answer to me!"

"Then what good are you?" Svetlana spat back. Turning back to her crew, she bellowed, "Athos, Martin, move out."

Athos's gaze swept the room. "Where's Hortence?"

"She disappeared. Likely pursuing her mother."

"Narci?"

"She's wounded. I'll get her," Svetlana said. She reached down to pick up Narci but fumbled with the Gem of the Seas. Had it been a simple gemstone, she could have placed it into a pocket. But this was a crown, and there was no good place on her person to stash it.

Except for atop her head.

Grimacing, Svetlana put on the crown holding the Gem of the Seas. The metal band to which the Gem and its neighbors were attached was cold and tight against her head. She slipped one end of the crown underneath the straps that held her monocular in place, pressing that end more closely to her scalp. It felt more secure, if still a bit unwieldy.

The overwhelming presence of the boiling seas resonated through every fiber of Svetlana's being, as though it had set her blood to boiling. She knew that with the simplest thought, she could calm the turbulent waters.

She also knew that doing so would ruin everything she and her crew had fought for.

Her mind filled with visions of a calm sea, with fish leaping across the surface and birds flying above. It almost felt like she was there, just above the surface of the water, with warm, balmy breezes ruffling her hair. A sense of tranquility pervaded her thoughts, and a smile sprang to her face unbidden.

She looked around, her sight filled with the prow of a ship larger than *The Silent Monsoon*, riding across the waves. Above her, sails billowed in the rigging, the normal balloons of airships nowhere to be seen. This was sailing, something she thought she would never get to do.

A glimmer of gold shimmered on her right side, and she turned to look at it. As she did, her smile slid away. She had no peripheral vision on her right side, on account of her blind eye.

"I'm dreaming," she muttered. Pushing aside thoughts of the Gem, of the oceans, and of anything that wasn't within her immediate field of actual vision, she focused on Narci and Athos, and she thought about the crew back on her ship, Annette, Indigo, Jo, Deliah, and Drassilis. Her thoughts spun farther, to Lar, Martin, and their family, Chickie, Hortence, and the other friends she had on platform cities across the world. She set her jaw and moved.

Scooping up Narci, she made her way to the door. She watched for any sign of Lady de Whittvy as she headed onto the deck.

Her forward movement was slowed abruptly by Athos and Martin facing off against another group of ghosts. "You signal Jo yet?" she asked Athos.

"No, we're a bit tied up." Athos jerked his chin in the direction of the flare gun he had tucked into his waistband.

"I can't fire it," Svetlana said. "I've got my hands full."

Hortence scrambled down the stairs, bowling through the ghosts in front of Athos and Martin, then smiled feebly at Svetlana. The mayor's daughter was bleeding from several shallow cuts on her face and arms, but other than that, she looked solid.

"Hortence, flare gun." Svetlana jerked her chin in Athos's direction.

Hortence's smile spread, and she dove for the flare gun, rolling over onto her back and peering up the stairs. "Fire in the hole," she said, sighting along the top of the gun.

Her good eye going wide, Svetlana twisted to the side, pulling Narci closer to her body to shield her.

The hiss of pain following Hortence's shot surprised Svetlana, and she turned her head to see who the mayor's daughter had shot.

Lady de Whittvy stood hunched over on the stairs above, a grimace of pain marring the parts of her face Svetlana could see.

Svetlana gloated for only a second before addressing Hortence. "I don't know if Jo could have seen that."

Hortence nodded, fumbling another flare from Athos's waistband, reloading the gun, and ascending the stairs. As the rest of the crew joined her on deck, she aimed it over the side of the ship to fire again. The second flare arced out and exploded off the starboard side of the ghost ship.

The Silent Monsoon drifted into position almost immediately, as if Jo had anticipated their need to leave the ship quickly. Annette stood ready with the gangplank. When she took in the scene on the ghost ship, she hurried back to the bridge. A moment later, *The Silent Monsoon* moved even closer to the ghost ship, almost near enough to bump it.

"Go, now," Svetlana said, nudging Athos.

Athos hurried across the gangplank, followed by Martin, and the two men took over for Annette, who had been bracing the wooden platform on her own.

Svetlana placed Narci on the gangplank next and pushed her as far across the wood as she could. Annette scooted out to meet her and brought Narci the rest of the way onboard the *Monsoon*.

"Hortence, it's time," Svetlana said, standing at the end of the gangplank.

Hortence nodded and began her retreat, but Lady de Whittvy had made her way to her daughter's position, lurking slightly behind her.

"Not again, you don't," Svetlana said, hurling her knife across the space. It struck Lady de Whittvy in the shoulder, drawing her attention away from Hortence and to Svetlana. As Hortence made her successful retreat, Svetlana smirked at Lady de Whittvy. "Goodbye, Vertiline."

Svetlana climbed onto the gangplank and crossed back to her ship.

CHAPTER EIGHTEEN

"She's stable," Annette said as soon as she entered the mess, before Svetlana had the chance to ask. "It'll take a while until she's back up to fighting speed, but she'll recover nicely."

Svetlana favored Annette with a smile and relaxed back into her chair. Hearing the good news about Narci's recovery was an enormous relief. It was almost better news than their recovery of the Gem of the Seas, though the latter was also a relief.

Athos and Jo, followed soon after by Indigo, Deliah, and Drassilis, filtered into the mess, leaving Martin and Hortence flying *The Silent Monsoon* across the Southern Sea, not bound for any particular location.

Svetlana took up her customary perch on the back of a chair to address her crew, the largest it had been in years. "Now that we have the Gem of the Seas, we need to make a decision. We know that if we wanted to, it could be used to tame the boiling sea. If we do that, though, all the platform cities will fall."

"Don't do that," Deliah said.

"We won't, don't worry," Svetlana replied. "There's a theory, advanced by Lady de Whittvy, that it might be possible to tame portions of the ocean, so we can pick and choose which platform cities stay in the air and which come down. That would give us time to evacuate the platform cities."

"That involves a bit too much power, if you ask me," Annette said, her brow furrowed. "Who are we to decide which platform cities are worthy and which aren't?"

"I think if we're going to start bringing platform cities down, the ultimate goal would be all of them," Athos said. "After evacuation."

"Might not work," Jo said.

Athos nodded. "She's right. We're basing this possibility on what Lady de Whittvy said, and she may have had her own motivations for suggesting it was possible."

"Agreed," Svetlana said. "Indy, Drassilis? Either of you want to weigh in on the possibilities so far?"

"Deliah is right. Don't do it," Indigo said.

"I do not believe myself qualified to weigh in on this decision, Captain Tereshchenko," Drassilis said.

"Why not?" Svetlana asked.

"There is a level of morality that I believe Mother left out of my programming. I am more inclined toward scientific experimentation, which suggests we should see what happens. This may be a relic of Mother's own thinking. So I will abstain from this decision."

"Excellently argued, Drassilis," Annette said, her eyes wide in astonishment. "Though you didn't say this directly, I will. The Gem is dangerous. Too many people would use it for their own ends. Even if we come up with an airtight plan for using it responsibly, that only lasts as long as we've got control of the Gem. It's far too easy to lose."

Svetlana nodded. "Bringing us neatly to option three. We destroy it." She held up her hand to forestall any argument before she was done. "Destruction ensures that no one else ever gets their hands on it and has to make this decision."

"What if destroying it stops the seas from boiling?" Jo asked.

"The first High General told me that the seas boiled before the Gem was created, and again after the Gem was lost. That suggests to me that if the Gem is destroyed, they'd still keep boiling."

"I can't confirm that, Captain," Annette said. "I've read histories of the time before the Boiling, but nothing that says there was a previous time when the oceans boiled."

"Has anyone ever explained why the oceans boiled?" Athos asked.

Annette shook her head. "The explanation has always been that the Gem was lost." Then she nodded slowly. "I suppose this gets into the question of 'why did the Gem exist?', and I don't have an answer for that. This is all uncharted territory."

Svetlana grinned. "We're pretty good at uncharted things. Indy, Deliah, Drassilis?"

"Smash it," Indigo said, Deliah nodding vigorously beside him.

"I will continue to abstain, Captain Tereshchenko," Drassilis said.

"Alright, vote then. Anyone in favor of stopping the boiling straight away?"

No hands raised.

"Anyone in favor of stopping some of the boiling after the platform cities have been evacuated?"

Again, no one raised a hand.

Svetlana chuckled softly. "Anyone in favor of smashing it into smithereens?"

Every member of the crew, save Drassilis, raised their hand.

A moment later, he joined in. "If it's going to be unanimous."

Svetlana nodded. "Thank you. Next step. How do we destroy it?"

"We could likely crush it beneath the diving bell," Drassilis suggested.

"And all get in and jump on it," Indigo suggested.

Drassilis shook his head decisively. "We will not all fit in the diving bell."

Indigo frowned. "Take turns?"

"Are we sure it can be crushed?" Athos asked. "I mean, it's a mystical magical thing. Shouldn't it need to be thrown into a volcano or something?"

"I don't trust volcanoes," Indigo said.

The remaining human crew looked at one another for a moment, their expressions making it clear that each was trying to parse what Indigo had just said, before Annette spoke up. "What makes them untrustworthy?"

"They're just fire. Might not destroy it completely."

"Bear in mind we've promised Dargon three-quarters of the treasure," Svetlana said, gesturing toward the Gem. "That's all we got, so we've got to give him his cut, or else we work for him for a year and a day."

"Who says we have to give him actual pieces?" Jo asked, her lips pressed into a smug grin.

"That's my girl," Athos said, giving Jo's shoulder a gentle squeeze. "I like this plan, Sveta. I'll even give up a mirror for the cause."

Svetlana considered what Dargon's reaction would be to receiving a box of powdered glass and chuckled. "Well, it does ensure he can't somehow put it all back together again."

"It isn't as though he has a way of testing it, is there?" Annette asked.

"Highly unlikely," Svetlana said.

"Crushed under the diving bell, then?" Athos asked.

Svetlana shrugged. "What are the other options?"

"Drassilis tried rolling over it. Didn't break," Indigo replied.

Athos held out his hands for the tiara.

Svetlana produced it from the interior pocket of her vest, which still bore traces of Narci's blood. "Don't put it on."

"Wasn't planning on it," Athos muttered. "I take it wearing it is a bad choice?"

"It makes things complicated," Svetlana replied.

Athos tested the metal band that held the fragments of crystals and glass together in his hands, frowning as he did. "We could put it on the winch and wind some rope over it, but I'm not sure that will do the trick either."

"Probably not," Indigo said. "Rope's too soft."

"If this thing is going to be so hard to break, what's it going to do to the floor of the hold if we crush it under the diving bell?" Svetlana asked. "Can we maybe not destroy the ship?"

"Drop it from the top of the cave in Bonebriar?" Indigo suggested, miming dropping something from the top of his reach to the mess table, which he smacked with his other hand. "Pa-chew!"

Athos flicked the center crystal with his fingernail, and it chimed, a mournful sound that sent a chill up Svetlana's spine. "It might work. It sounds like glass."

"It's not just glass," Svetlana said. "We'll try the diving bell. On the street in Bonebriar. We can use the pulleys to pick it up and drop it down until the pieces are small enough."

"With us inside?" Indigo asked.

"Do you really want to ride inside the diving bell, Indy?" Svetlana asked.

Indigo considered for a moment, then shook his head. "Another time."

~

Indigo and Deliah held a tarp between the two of them, maneuvering beneath the suspended diving bell. A few of the residents of Bonebriar had come out to watch this spectacle, all of them looking confused as to what was going on outside Lady de Whittvy's former home.

Athos and Drassilis manned the pulley system that held the diving bell aloft, with Athos suggesting occasional adjustments to the teenagers.

Svetlana, and the remainder of her crew, plus their current guests, stood to one side, watching with considerably more interest and knowledge than the residents of Bonebriar. She held a plain canvas bag containing the Gem of the Seas in one hand. If it could be destroyed, a thin layer of canvas wouldn't protect it from the weight of the diving bell, but it would keep it from prying eyes.

"I know it's not my place to intrude, but you're sure about this?" Martin asked.

"Positive," Svetlana said. "Though I'll hear you out if you have a suggestion."

Martin shook his head. "I don't, not really. I just hate seeing something like that go to waste."

"You're not the only one who will," Svetlana replied. "The problem is, there are some people who would stop at nothing to get their hands on this, and I can't risk my crew being forever on the run to protect it."

"We could lock it up somewhere," Martin suggested.

"Wherever we put it would never be safe. I don't want to put that on anyone's head."

"Then I'll rescind my suggestion," Martin said.

"Good," Svetlana said, grinning at him. "Glad to be on the same page."

Athos waved to the assembled crew, drawing their attention. "Jo! Come over here. You get the first drop!"

Jo looked at Svetlana, brow furrowed, pointing to her own chest.

"We voted," Svetlana said. "For your valor and all that. And because Athos asked me nicely."

A faint blush danced across Jo's cheeks, gone almost before Svetlana was certain she'd seen it, and Jo hurried to join Athos.

Svetlana held the bag containing the Gem of the Seas in both hands for a moment. She couldn't be sure this was going to work, but they had to try. She approached the tarp, looking at the diving bell warily, and then set the bag in what appeared to be the direct center beneath the heavy capsule, moving off the tarp as soon as it was in place.

"Here goes nothing," Athos called out.

Jo pulled a lever, and the diving bell plummeted to the ground. A crunching sound followed, and the entire crew let out a cheer.

Athos moved the lever back to its starting position while Drassilis started the winch to raise the diving bell back above the street.

As soon as there was enough clearance, Indigo darted forward and grabbed the bag, peering inside. "Not smashed."

Svetlana joined him and looked into the bag. Portions of the crystals had chipped off, but the central stone was still whole. Shrugging, she said, "We'll keep trying until it works." She repositioned the bag beneath the diving bell and retreated to the place where the crew stood.

"Who gets second drop?" Annette asked.

"Drassilis," Svetlana said. "Then Hortence, then Deliah. Then Narci if she's up for it. Martin, do you want a turn?"

Martin shrugged. "If it's going to take all of us dropping it, then sure, I'll take a turn."

"Sveta, Jo wants you to go next," Athos called out.

Svetlana looked toward her first mate and pilot, alongside Lady de Whittvy's automaton. "I have the order all figured out."

"She thinks you're the one with the biggest grudge against the thing, and maybe that's its own kind of magic," Athos said, glancing at Jo. "Right?"

Jo nodded, gesturing to the lever.

"You are the captain, Captain," Annette said.

Svetlana wasn't convinced, but she shrugged. "Alright, sure."

With everything in order, Svetlana took her position at the lever, ready to drop the diving bell.

"Think how much you want it gone," Jo whispered.

Recalling how the Gem had attempted to get her to use it, Svetlana nodded and pulled the lever.

The resultant sound was a clear shattering that rung like crystal struck with a hard object.

Again, Athos and Drassilis went to work resetting the pulley system, and Indigo reached beneath the diving bell. This time, though, the bag had clearly been flattened. The mechanic grinned as he looked inside. "Smithereens!"

Svetlana joined him. The Gem of the Seas and the other stones that had surrounded it were little more than glittering shards, the metal band that had held them together now flattened. She glanced up at Jo and smiled. "That did it."

Once the diving bell was swinging overhead, Svetlana knelt and poured the remains of the Gem of the Seas onto the center of the tarp. "One last thing we need to do." Using her knife, she separated the shattered remains into four equal piles, then pushed three of those piles back into a single one. "That's three-quarters of the Gem of the Seas. We need a comparable amount of something that can match the size of that pile."

"Some mirrors, maybe some cheap jewelry?" Athos suggested.

Svetlana grinned. "Perfect. That and a wooden box, and we've got our three-quarters for Dargon."

~

Despite Indigo's distrust of the destructive capability of volcanoes, they had proven to be useful disposal locations for fragments of the now shattered Gem of the Seas. They'd flown throughout the Southern Sea, distributing most of the pieces of crushed Gem there, but saving some for their future journeys in the north, so all the pieces wouldn't be concentrated too closely together.

Now Svetlana carried a wooden box filled with entirely different fragments of glass and gemstones tucked under her arm as she awaited her audience with Dargon. Guaa had promised the delay wouldn't be long, and Svetlana imagined Dargon would be desperate to end whatever meeting he had been in, in order to see what his treasure would be.

Guaa poked her head out from the audience chamber, her gaze fixed on the box more than Svetlana herself. "He's ready for you."

Svetlana smiled and walked in, ignoring the stares and whispers of Dargon's court.

For his part, Dargon sat upright in his throne, rather than his normal casual sprawl across it. He eyed the box, then looked at Svetlana, arching one eyebrow. "That's it?"

Svetlana stopped in front of him and opened the box so he could see the shimmering shards that filled it. "Your seventy-five percent."

"What in the bloody abyss am I to do with your ... glitter?" Dargon asked, his voice almost a growl.

"This is what we have," Svetlana said, pausing as she closed the box. "So far, at least."

"So far?" Dargon asked, his shoulders relaxing a touch.

Svetlana handed him the box as she launched into her pitch. "The sea caves contain the Last Emperor's Hoard, in its entirety. We didn't have the opportunity to collect it all. We're willing to make a second expedition, now that we're fairly certain we won't face opposition this time. And seventy-five percent of what's down there should make up for our initial poor showing."

With a soft chuckle, Dargon said, "Now that sounds more like it. But perhaps I should send Guaa with you to make sure it doesn't all come back in pieces."

"Suit yourself," Svetlana said, "but we could certainly use something more than what we cobbled together to get down there last time. I'm hopeful that whatever the ghosts did to destabilize the air supply will have gone back to normal now ... well, for a definition of normal."

"More assistance, eh?" Dargon said, steepling his fingers. "That might necessitate more of the treasure."

"We're technically square, you and I," Svetlana said.

Dargon's eyes narrowed. "How do you figure?"

Svetlana gestured at the box. "We brought you exactly seventy-five percent of what we retrieved, at substantial peril to me and Athos." She shrugged. "Let's be honest—in shards is the only way we could have split that treasure."

"Wasn't it some sort of a string of gems?" Guaa asked, speaking up for the first time.

"Crown, actually," Svetlana replied. "And only the center stone had any value at all. The rest were just quartz crystals."

"Then she's right, sir," Guaa said. "You're square."

Svetlana smiled at Guaa. "What I'm proposing would be more of a partnership, which makes seventy-five percent more than generous."

Dargon smirked but nodded. "Alright, I'll support your little venture with equipment and crew for seventy-five percent of the takings. Agreed?" He extended his hand to Svetlana.

Svetlana stepped forward and shook his hand. "Agreed."

~

The Silent Monsoon took off from the Unfathomed Enclave loaded down with additional crew and equipment loaned to them by Dargon. Most of his people were in the cargo hold, but they'd also agreed to take shifts on maintaining the steam reserves, which meant that for the first time in a long time, Svetlana had her entire crew on the bridge at once.

Athos and Jo flew the ship side by side, communicating mostly by gestures and nudges. Jo was finally able to speak more than a few brief sentences without pain, but the two of them almost seemed to communicate better without words. When they caught each other's gaze, they smiled and laughed, rather than the bickering that had so often marred their previous relationship. They seemed like they were finally happy.

Hortence, who was flying with the crew for the time being, stood at the prow of the ship, spyglass in hand. She looked less like a mayor's daughter and more like the bunch of pirates she'd thrown her lot in with. She also looked content for the first time since Svetlana had met her, and Svetlana wondered if that had more to do with the environment or with knowing her mother was unlikely to trouble her further.

Annette had brought Narci up to the bridge, sat her in a chair and ordered her not to move. But despite these strictures, Narci seemed to be enjoying herself, basking in the autumn sunlight and watching the clouds go by. It would be a month or so before she was up for helping out on the crew, but Svetlana was willing to give her a pass for the time being.

Meanwhile, Indigo, Deliah, and Drassilis played some sort of game that involved the two teenagers laughing a lot and Drassilis occasionally making outlandish guesses about what they were doing. Svetlana had only caught snippets of their conversation, and it seemed to be about as nonsensical as it could possibly be, which certainly confused the automaton's logical and unnuanced mind.

Svetlana leaned against the steering console, taking it all in, as Annette joined her.

"So, boiling seas forever?" Annette asked.

Svetlana nodded. "Maybe not what we thought we wanted, but I think it's for the best in the long run."

"A lot of people are safer for it, that's for certain," Annette said, nodding in agreement.

"It's also an element of job security, when it comes down to it," Svetlana said.

"How do you figure?"

"I don't know how to sail," Svetlana said, smiling. "Never needed to learn how. But I do know how to fly. If people could sail again, who would need airship pirates?"

ACKNOWLEDGEMENTS

It's taken a little longer than I hoped, but I'm pleased to say that I've finally completed my first trilogy. It's a great feeling of accomplishment for me, but it also couldn't have happened without help.

Thanks to Christine and Alisha, who are the reasons why this book exists. Thanks for getting me started on the journey! Thanks to the best beta reader a woman could ever want, my sister-from-another-mister, Amanda R., for literally reading this book in less than 24 hours and having super useful feedback! Thanks to Torchy, Andrew, and Yi-Mei. You may not remember, but you gave me city names that wound up in my world. I only wish I could have snuck more of them in here, but I'll just have to save those for another world.

Thanks to Nate, Torrey, Dietrich, Sarah, and Jeremy for being the best writing cheerleaders and random question helpers. Jeremy has still not lost his naming privileges, and he remains the reason why I can write as much as I do. Thank you for encouraging and supporting me through this whole process and stepping up to make this book a reality.

And finally, thanks to everyone who's been following along on this ride. Authors write to get the ideas out of their heads, but they also need readers to enjoy their ideas. Thanks for letting me know that you were excited by what you'd already read, and that you wanted more! *The Silent Monsoon* couldn't have flown as far as she did without your support!

ABOUT THE AUTHOR

Dawn Vogel's academic background is in history, so it's not surprising that much of her fiction is set in earlier times. By day, she edits reports for historians and archaeologists. In her alleged spare time, she runs a craft business, co-edits *Mad Scientist Journal*, and tries to find time for writing. She is a member of Broad Universe, SFWA, and Codex Writers. She lives in Seattle with her husband, author Jeremy Zimmerman, and their herd of cats. Visit her at http://historythatneverwas.com.